THE COMING

Daniel Black

ST. MARTIN'S PRESS

NEW YORK

THE COMING. Copyright © 2015 by Daniel Black. All rights reserved. Printed in the United States of America. For information, address St. Martin's Press, 175 Fifth Avenue, New York, N.Y. 10010.

www.stmartins.com

ISBN 978-1-250-09862-7 (trade paperback)
ISBN 978-1-4668-9067-1 (e-book)

Our books may be purchased in bulk for promotional, educational, or business use. Please contact your local bookseller or the Macmillan Corporate and Premium Sales Department at 1-800-221-7945, extension 5442, or by e-mail at MacmillanSpecialMarkets@macmillan.com.

First Edition: October 2015

P1

This book is dedicated to the memory and celebration of African souls lost in the Atlantic Ocean. We have not forgotten you. You are our strength. We, your children, exalt you and sing of your glory forever. This is also for those who reached land but never made it home. Your struggle was not in vain. We remember you. We name our children after you. We travel to Mother Africa and take you with us. You are home again.

It was the coming that was bad. . . .

—**Sonia Sanchez**

PART I

We didn't know we wouldn't return. We simply believed some terrible calamity had befallen us, that our Gods had let tragedy come because we had not honored them. But we were wrong.

We were warriors and hunters, poets and jali, farmers and soothsayers. We were magicians and healers, artisans and thinkers, writers and dancers. We were fathers and mothers, sisters and brothers, cousins and kinsmen. We were lovers. And we were home. We loved the land and it loved us. We were black like the land, and kissed by the sun. We knew our strengths and our frailties, and we knew much needed improvement. But we were home.

We were the Fon, the Ibo, the Hausa, the Ashanti, the Mandinka, the Ewe, the Tiv, and the Ga. We were the Fante, the Fulani, the Ijaw, the Mende, the Wolof, the Yoruba, the BaKongo, and the Mbundu. We were the Serere, the Akan, the Bambara and the Bassa. And we were proud. We knew our ancestors by name. They knew our names: Kwesi, Lusati, Lutalo, Yejide, Chinasa, Obrafo, Yaasantewa, Mawu, Ombeni, Chinsera, and Ubongo. We were Fatou, Folami, Olumide, Amalu, Ifetayo, Kacela, Shamba, and Sowande. And each name has a meaning: "He who opens ways." "She comes softly like the rain, yet floods the rivers." "I am my father's loved one, my mother's precious one who makes everything all right." "She is a hunter, gathering sweet words for us all." "Mother of the universe who represents great wisdom." "Born on Sunday." "Born on Tuesday." "Born on Friday." "This child is priceless." Our names told us who we were. They told us why we'd been sent. What was expected of us. We were not confused. We were not ashamed. We were not perfect, but we were excellent.

And we were content. Our lives had meaning. Some had completed our initiations, some were beginning our initiations. Through this process, we became students of the universe. We learned the healing herbs of the forest. We learned the activity of the ants on the hills. We learned the difference between the sky and the heavens. We learned the difference between the brain and the mind. We were schooled. We were scolded. We were honored. We were praised. We were reprimanded. But we were home.

Among us lived every spirit conceivable. Men who loved women, women who loved men. Women who loved women, men who loved men. These were not choices but life assignments. Everyone had one. There were people who could read the signs in the heavens.

People who lived both here and beyond. People who could hear the voice of God. People who understood the makings of the universe. People who interpreted the song of the wind. People who never bore children, but raised everyone. People who wept when others wept. People who inspired by words alone. People who told stories and never became redundant. People who walked the forest at night without fear. People who healed with their hands. People who brought forth fruit from the land. People who carved masks with perfect precision. People whose joy was helping other people. People who stood guard over our spirits.

There were other people, too. People who talked too much. People who loved lies more than truth. People who tampered with evil. People who wouldn't work. People who were consumed with jealousy. Manipulation. Deceit. Scorn. People who held grudges for far too long. People who sowed discord in the community. People who tore families apart with dissension. People with poor discretion. People with malnourished minds. And so on. We were wonderful, but we were not flawless. We knew excellence because we knew failure. We were human beings.

We'd built kingdoms that lived in legend. Luanda, Kissi, Temne, and Dahomey all boasted kings, governors, and organizational documents that told the world how to administrate large numbers of people. Oyo stood as the military capital of the world. It trained soldiers with such precision that most enemies surrendered to avoid being decimated. Gola, Kongo, and Lunda inspired neighbors with artistic displays of dance, poetry, and kente weaving unequaled anywhere in the region. The nations of Fula, Mande, Susu, and Vili built wealth by trading fish from nearby rivers and lakes. Some kingdoms, however, gained power at the hands of the poor. Those of non-royal birth often found themselves in the service of royalty. Fata Jallon thrived precisely because the majority of its citizens surrendered their goods to the ruling regime. This was not rare. We were not pleased. Still, we were home.

We were people who loved balance. The most attractive girl among us was neither fat nor thin. We admired a mid-size frame, carried by one of enormous confidence. Too much flesh meant one was prone to laziness; too little meant one's family could not provide. We shunned extremities. We welcomed the rain just as we celebrated the sun. We beckoned the night much as we summoned the dawn. We slept as much as we worked. We laughed as much as we wept. We birthed as often as we buried. This was life. Everything in its time.

We lived off the land. Cassava and rice grew in great abundance. We also ate eggplant, okra, tomatoes, chickpeas, plantain, and always fufu or kenkey or garri. Our main dishes were groundnut stew, jollof rice, smoked fish and onions, yassa, maafe, and sometimes bushmeat. We didn't know what particular animal this was. Elders teased us about it being wild boar or rat. We tried to avoid it, yet occasionally hunger would not be denied. For breakfast, we ate a type of rice porridge or kooko, but often we simply ate what was left from the previous evening. We seasoned with peppers of every kind, onions, cumin, garlic, coconut oil, black pepper, salt, cinnamon, cloves, and thyme. A master cook was praised and highly sought after among our people. She would have many suitors, and her bride price would be exorbitant. Still, young men fought for her hand, convinced that life with such a woman would be glorious. And it usually was—if for the belly alone.

We were people of the same land, but we were not identical. Indeed, we were every shade conceivable. Some bore the color of the black leopard. Some, the rusty brown of the earth. Some glimmered golden like grains of sand. Some shared the dull gray of tree bark. Some appeared reddish, as if hewn from rocks and stones of the hills. Our bodies reflected our environment. The hair of those from Gabon twisted and coiled like the viper. From every region of land, we braided and decorated our hair, then strutted through our villages, showing off proud crowns. From our ears hung rings that whistled in the wind. In our broad noses we placed artifacts of wood and iron that reminded us of the bounty of our land. In ceremony, we painted high cheekbones, protruding lips, and bulbous eyes that emphasized our value for spiritual sight and levels of knowing. We all adorned ourselves, to one degree or another, because we loved ourselves.

We believed in one God. We believed in lesser gods. We believed we looked like our gods. We believed they lived among us, whispering secrets into our hearts and minds. We believed that life was everlasting. That our souls were ancient. That there was no beginning, no ending. Only change and growth. That all life was connected: animals, trees, water, earth. Everything had energy. We studied these elements in search of ourselves.

We sat in the center of the village, beneath the starry sky, listening to elders boast of our heroes. Warriors who fought thirty men by themselves and came home victorious. Hunters who, with knives and bows, captured enough meat to feed a thousand. Fishermen who returned from the waters with enough fish to feed the entire village. Farmers whose harvest could've fed the world. The stories made us proud. The uninitiated longed to serve and be celebrated in this way. As sleep came on, we returned home and rested until the rooster crowed, beckoning us into a new day.

Our days were filled with work. Carving drums from the baobab tree. Smelting iron, copper, and gold for jewelry and ornamentation. Weaving cloth, strand by precious strand, until bolts of brilliant, multicolored material lay ready for use. Cleaning homes and animal pens. Herding goats, cows, and lambs. Washing clothes in nearby streams. Transporting water from rivers and lakes. Weeding and tending gardens for sustenance and market. Gathering wood and trees for building and cooking. Rearing children and comforting the old. Work was the price we paid for our breath. The lazy were shunned and reprimanded.

Often, after work, we danced. Tired as we were, we could not resist the call of the drums. Our movements mimicked everyday life. Some gestures imitated the casting of nets in the waters. Some, the pounding of yam. Some, the planting of seeds. Some, the meshing of bodies in the creation of life. And some, the quiet stealth of hunters in the forest. Our bodies swayed like the branches of trees, and pulsated, back and forth, like moving waters. We were in constant motion. At times, our dance was slow and mystical like the night; other times, wild and frenzied like fierce, rushing wind. We mimicked animals, too. Our hands and hips twisted with the grace of the gazelle. We shuffled our feet like mighty cheetahs. Our arms, like a monkey's, rotated in opposite directions, then hung loose and limber at our sides. We slung our heads back and pranced in circles like the guinea fowl. And every now and then we stomped with the weight and power of elephants until the earth vibrated beneath us. For everything, we danced: funerals, births, deaths, weddings, harvest, planting, initiation, war. We named our dances kuku, manjani, soli, soko, tiriba, adowa, abgekor, and gota. We named them kete, mouwa, doudumba, kakilambe, bawa, and sorsornnet. Everywhere we lived, we danced. We told our stories through dance. We were never stagnant. Even in sleep, our spirits met and mingled in movement. Those who couldn't dance danced anyway. Our pride was in the majesty of our moving forms.

And after dancing, we sat at the feet of our elders and absorbed wisdom like tilled earth absorbs rain. We were taught the values of honesty and integrity, hard work and discipline. We heard stories of lazy farmers who planted crops but failed to weed them and consequently harvested very little. We heard stories of children who lied so often that, soon, no one believed anything they said. We heard stories of pretty women who became self-absorbed and ended up alone. We heard stories of ants that, in their diligence, never let others deflect them from their mission. We were told to beware people who boasted about themselves. We were told never, ever, to eat without first giving thanks. We were told to respect life and all life forms. Day and night, our heads were filled with insight enough to last a lifetime. Every child heard it. We had no choice. In this way, they gave us the tools of wisdom.

Yet, at times, we didn't use it. Our imperfections, over seasons, became weaknesses that contributed to our demise. We were arrogant, often, about our achievements. Women were sometimes silenced during public gatherings. Some of our men drank too much. We didn't always share our harvest the way we should have. Elders were increasingly neglected. We spoke more proverbs than we lived. We favored some citizens over others. We punished harshly those we did not prefer. We skipped rituals for no good reason. We made excuses, at times, for things we'd simply failed to do. We gossiped about our neighbors. We even disobeyed our sacred laws. Some hunters slaughtered game in excess, knowing full well that such was against the pleasure of the gods. Still, they were often heralded as great men of valor. Their plenty became the measure of manhood, eroding our moral consciousness and making us gluttonous lovers of superfluous things. We knew better. We'd been taught the way of harmony and balance. Yet, often, we measured our worth not by what we had but by what our neighbors had, so the disease of greed spread among us. At first it was not discernible, but slowly it seeped into our hearts, assuring that, one day, we'd trade cultural traditions and personal integrity for the luster of material gain.

That day arrived.

We traded blindly with those from every corner of the earth. The yellow man, the reddish brown, the tan. Every man wanted what he did not have. In exchange for gold and ivory, they gave us sweet spices and guns. Some of the traders never went home. They were impressed by our ways, by how our children relished the company of elders, by how our healers cured diseases, often without medicine. They spoke the names of their countries: England, Portugal, Spain, France, The Netherlands. We wondered what those nations were like. If, like us, men hunted while women planted crops and cared for children. Or if, in their villages, some painted and decorated their bodies. We didn't know. No pale man bore the marks of his tribe. Some told of their people and cultural ways that were unlike our own. They spoke of beasts we did not know and foods we'd never heard of. They showed us currency that resembled mere pieces of paper, and flat, round stones they called coins. Their children played strange games with strange objects, but, like us, they played all the same. We were definitely different people, but on the surface, it seemed, very much the same.

We also wondered if, perhaps, back in their lands they

performed rituals to honor their dead. When we mentioned ours, they seemed not to understand how the two, the living and the not-living, coexisted. We laughed at first, sure that they were mocking us, since everyone knows that life transcends all realms, but once we discovered their seriousness, we froze in horror.

Then came the disaster.

With open arms, we embraced those who looked nothing like us, assuming all life honors life.

We were wrong.

In the end, we fed and strengthened our own captors. We cannot claim naiveté. We cannot say we were people undeveloped. We cannot say there were no signs. We can say only that we did not heed them. Sound wisdom was as common to us as the evening breeze. We scoffed and shrugged at elders' forewarning of a time of great tragedy and chaos. We did not believe them. We had learned to ignore our own gods. To take their goodness for granted. To believe that because of them, we were immune to external attack. So we did not hear them. We heard only what we sought to hear. Now we hear it all, echoing in our regretful memories.

If only we could have seen into the future, we might have avoided the onslaught. Most of us had no such powers. The few who did, the seers and sages, we dismissed. They were always speaking of things to come, warning of impending disasters that rarely came to pass. At least in our lifetime. Now we know that prophesies come to one generation and materialize in another. If only we had listened. If only we had had more disciplined ears. We did not.

We blamed ourselves. We blamed our gods. We blamed each other. But there was no one to blame. Only shame to bear. And pity. Great pity. That a people so strong had missed so many clues. The forests whispered it. The birds chirped it. The trees waved it. The antelope danced it. The tall grass swayed it. The lions roared it. The elders said it, over and over. "Beware! Seek not the thing you do not need. Greed destroys wisdom. Let *just* enough be enough." We were too blessed. Our abundance suggested immortality, so we stopped searching for invisible things. Our mothers had worked so hard that we did not have to. Our fathers had killed enough game that their sons hardly knew the hunt. We didn't know then what we know now: A life of leisure destroys a child. When there's nothing to work for, there's nothing to gain, nothing to die for. So we had to die that we might live again.

And that's what we did. We died. By the thousands and hundreds of thousands. We'd never seen such unjustifiable violence. Bloody bodies lying prostrate across the earth as if pleading for forgiveness. Those who survived did not mourn. There was no time. The loss was too great. We still have not mourned. We still have no time. We remember, but we have not mourned.

Death came quickly. It came unannounced. It came cloaked in our own multicolored garb. It came white as clouds, smiling as if it loved us. It came in the darkness of night while we were laughing and talking with ancestors. It came in legions with guns and ammunition too powerful for us to battle. It came like the monsoon winds. It came like a flood. It came with earthshaking force we could not control. It came under the authority of nations we did not know. It came with men whose absent wives benefited from their husbands' despicable behavior. It came with men whose children would one day inherit their fathers' legacy of violence and wealth ill gained. It came to strip the land of its glory. It came to thousands and hundreds of thousands without sympathy for our loss. It came with impaled brutality. It came to scatter children's blood-soaked bodies about the earth, thus fertilizing dry, yearning soil. It came to teach us we were brothers.

This was The Coming.

. . .

Some were taken by surprise. Some were killed on the

spot. Some were taken in their sleep. Some were ambushed in the forest. Some were tricked into believing they were going for a walk. Some, consumed with hatred, were caught off guard. Some were inebriated. Some were too lazy to fight. Some were busy settling communal affairs. Some were nursing wounds inflicted by spouses. Some were telling children bedtime stories of talking spiders. Some were beating drums to warn others. Most were not listening. When the drums fell silent, it was too late. Our destruction was complete. An entire village razed in one solitary cycle of the sun and moon.

They destroyed our homes and forced our leaving. They bound us with chains of heavy iron. Elders were rendered mute and lifeless. Babies deprived of life's knowing. All we could do was wonder. We did not speak. There was nothing to say. In those moments we heard our elders' warnings. And we understood. We knew they loved us now, far more than we had understood before. But they could not hear our cries, our pleas of lament. Not with the ears of the living. So, one by one, they took us away.

They seized our farmers first. Those who knew the land, the earth, the ingredients of the soil. Those who heard its rumble, felt its movement, understood its seasons. Those who knew seeds and germination, plant spacing and harvesting. Those who walked barefoot upon the soil in homage to its life-sustaining power. They took them first. It was no accident. They would farm again in a new world, feeding a nation committed to their degradation.

Then they took our healers. They were not hard to find. Most days, they lingered about the village, repairing bodies and minds too troubled to heal alone. They had learned from us the value of our healers. They knew that, without them, we were weak, vulnerable people. If they took our healers, they must've assumed, they also took our ability to mend ourselves. They were right. So they captured our healers that we might not rebound. Villages of frightened, wounded people, without medicine men and women, would take centuries to restore. They knew this. Their strategy was as calculated as the hyenas' attack. Without shamans, who would usher life back into our suffering souls? Who would reassure us that Death had not come to stay? Who would cleanse the forest and the land of poisonous energy brought by evildoers? We didn't know. What we knew was that our wounds would fester for a lifetime without someone to cure them. In a day, panic and uncertainty became our way. Our pride deteriorated into fractured, deep-seated insecurities.

Next, they took our jali, that our stories might not be told. After them, the warriors, that our collective strength might be diminished. Then they bound the artists, who had told us we were beautiful. They chained and muted orators and teachers to stop the flow of inspiration and abort the belief that we were gods. They murdered gate-keepers on the spot since, at their word, multitudes of ancestors would've come. They would've come! But they were never called. And, finally, they slaughtered those whose gifts were less visible, although to us no less valuable: keepers of knowledge, masters of the spirit, gurus of assistance, guardians of order and balance. In the end, they stole away everyone and everything that made us strong.

This was The Coming.

We marched quickly. We marched through forests. We marched over hills and valleys. We marched through hot, desert land. We marched alongside waterfalls and brooks, which, the day before, had quenched our thirsts. We marched through high grass. We marched on barren earth. We marched past monkeys that dashed through trees, screeching and squealing with confusion. We marched past giraffes whose frantically swiveling heads told us to never give up the fight. We marched past lions roaring anxiously in the distance. We marched past anthills wherein frightened ants scrambled hysterically, then vanished out of sight. We marched past gardens sprouted, but not tilled. We marched past neighboring villages we thought we despised. We marched past sights of rituals where we'd known spirit possession and healing. We marched past communal huts where government officials once met to solve collective dilemmas. We marched past people we did not know. We marched through regions we had never seen. We marched until some of us died. They were unchained and tossed aside. There are no markers to commemorate them. Of this we are sure. We marched and we marched, from the rising till the setting of the sun. Then we collapsed and the moon gave us ease. But at the sun's rising, we marched some more.

Soon we heard the roar of the river. We knew its sound. It had lived among us for as long as we'd been there. We believed, just as before, that its lullaby would calm our souls. Yet, this time, its disquiet was of warning, not welcome. It told of a life that awaited, a reality filled with death and despair. It encouraged our escape, although this was hardly possible. A few, however, heard and heeded the call. How they slipped their chains we do not know, but they leapt, with the height of the impala, across tall grass until they disappeared into the past from which we had come. The rest of us, the fateful ones, continued marching until the river's call deafened. We could not escape. The river was our kinsman, but it could not save us. It could not help us. Not this time.

In our own riverboats they took us, until the river

flowed into the mouth of The Great Mother. Her reach was far and wide, her spirit turbulent. Our boats navigated carefully across her watery terrain and rested where the waters licked the shore. Then we were taken into stone structures where we were packed like herded goats. The space was damp and musty and hot, and there were no windows—only occasional cracks in walls where salty wind blew in and dried our skin, leaving us itchy and miserable. So many crowded into such a small space. We could hardly sit or move. Every hour, someone died. Whether from suffocation or illness, we watched people vanish without ceremony or burial. Sounds of suffering and sorrow became our daily song as bodies deteriorated before our very eyes. Moans, grunts, sighs, and cries echoed throughout holding pens like pleas of desperate, trapped beasts. We didn't know what to do. Different pale men stood guard over us now They were not the ones who had captured us. Perhaps one had traded us to the other. All we knew for sure was that home was some distant place, and we were losing faith we'd ever see it again.

Day turned to night, and our misery multiplied. By the hundreds, we bowed our heads and grieved. Some tried to relive our capture, speaking aloud names of those left behind or killed. Some even admitted, beneath their breaths, that they'd sensed danger, but ignored it. They never forgave themselves. Others fainted from heat and heart exhaustion. They collapsed as if all life had been drained from them. A few touched these limp bodies sympathetically, but no one attended them. We didn't have the strength. It was all we could do simply to survive.

Most children had been killed or left behind, but a few lingered among us. Their faces of terror and panic never left our consciousness. Trembling and shivering with eyes wide open, they clung like leeches to frantic mothers and fathers who wanted only to protect them. But they could not. We knew these children wouldn't last. Their precious, fragile lives would be sacrificed to disease, suffocation, or distress. Only the strong would survive. And children are never that strong.

There were different compartments, or so it seemed. We heard voices outside of our area. Mostly names being shouted in hopes of a response. There was usually no response. Once, though, a man's heavy, quivering voice bellowed through the air, "Shamba! Shamba! Shamba!" We waited, prepared to weep along when no answer came. But within seconds, a young, strong, male voice returned, "Baba! Baba Shamba!" and we wept still, but for the grace of the gods. This was not usual. It would not happen again.

We were days in those holding pens, waiting for our future to unfold. Captors sat a bucket of lukewarm water in the center of the floor each day, and within seconds of their leave, it was gone. Most never tasted it. There were more than a hundred of us packed together in that small room, and there was never enough water to go around. For food, they threw us half-rotten fruit and discarded portions of whatever they'd eaten. It was always minimal. Only a few tasted that, too. Even children were neglected.

Some days, they took hundreds away while the rest of us continued waiting. Suffering. Longing. Hoping captors would have a change of heart and set us free. They never did. Instead, we sat in those cells for weeks and months at a time. Rancid diseases claimed many lives. Others died from pain deep in the soul. A few wept until tears ran dry. We could scarcely sigh without our breath tickling the neck of a kinsman, so most of us bowed our heads and held our breath. We called for warriors who never came. We were naked and ashamed.

We cannot recall their names, the departed. We can only hear, ringing in our memories, the wailing of a people too broken to heal. A woman whose language we could not discern tried to encourage us. We felt the upsurge in her tone, and for a time her power prevailed, yet after days and nights in the sweltering heat, pleading continuously, she collapsed, exasperated. She simply could not bear our burdens alone. Her voice went silent. She left us altogether—left her body right in our midst, and walked proudly into the next realm. We heard her in our sleep, reminding us who we were and telling us to never lose hope. Someone later said her name was Elewechi, which means, "Do nothing unless God decides."

There were men, too, in those cells, fighting for our survival, intent to prove themselves men. They tried to escape, but they could not. They screamed and flailed their arms, like children with the fits, and slung their bodies onto the earth, kicking and shouting all the while. Most of us turned away. Our eyes avoided their eyes, that we might not see the depth of their agony. That was the only way we knew to love them.

This was The Coming.

· · ·

We saw the ships before they saw us. Narrow cracks in stonewalls allowed us to breathe and watch big vessels approach. Leaning neither to the right nor the left, they glided along the water's surface with remarkable balance and quiet ease. We were astonished that such big boats did not sink. Tall poles stood in the middle of them, with large blocks of white cloth waving at the top, guiding them into what would become familiar waters. We would later learn the names of these vessels: *The Hope, The Lord Ligonier, The Mary, The Brookes, The Henry of London, The*

Hannibal of London, The Good Ship Jesus, The Henrietta Marie, The Charleston, The Arabella, The Katherine, The Green Dragon and so many others. They could not come ashore. They were too big. So our riverboats took us to them.

On board ships, captors did not love us. We knew this. But they wanted us. For something vile, something wrong, something that would diminish the supplier while exalting the supplied. Where we were going we did not know. Where our gods had gone we did not know. We called them, over and over again, but the wind returned only silence. Some jumped overboard, into the depths of the Great Mother, but with hands and feet bound, their struggling forms sank instantly into the dark water. Captors did not weep. They seemed, instead, to harbor anger that we did not want to go with them. Their words we could not understand.

They picked through us like an assortment of fruit, choosing whom they preferred. They scattered and melded tribes. One of our own, a man they called Frank, made this possible. He knew us. He knew our marks. We knew his. He knew what would break our spirits. And he enjoyed doing so. With his help, they shuffled us belowdecks into the big bellies of the boats. They packed us on our sides in rows and lines, arching our bodies to fit into narrow chambers. Sometimes they took us all with no regard for human comfort. Some, chained with the willing and unwilling, jumped into the water, trying, once again, to swim away, but they either died, were captured, or killed. We knew not where we were going. But we knew we were not going home.

One by one, men and women were stacked like books on a shelf. Hundreds lay this way, in the big boat's belly, weeping silently for a home we'd never see again. In lucid moments, we wondered who these people were—not in flesh, but in spirit—and how, in good conscience, they could treat us this way. In other moments we talked to silent gods. *Oshun? Obatala? Yemaya? Allah? Can you hear us?* They did not reply.

Some women were taken elsewhere. We learned later that they were not shackled, as we were, yet in their freedom they were not free. Their bodies serviced the captors' pleasure, warming frigid beds and encasing throbbing penises. We heard the shrieks of our daughters, mothers, sisters, aunts, their screams, their piercing cries, not of excitement and joy, but of horror and pain as unwelcomed flesh divided their souls. These were our women, and we could not help them.

Wails and cries intensified during the night. We were shrouded in darkness. This was not like our nights, with brilliant stars so close you could practically reach up and touch them, this was darkness so black, so complete, it swallowed us whole. We could see nothing. Even the body to which we were chained became invisible in the deep purple blackness.

Above and below, feces, urine, menstrual blood, mucus, and death surrounded us, multiplying by the hour. The stench nauseated. Our only relief was to vomit, but then our bellies were emptied of the few nutrients it held. We begged Death to come and for some, it came. For others, not at all. We'd never summoned Death before, never beckoned its power, its premature arrival, never desired its unwelcomed stay. Now, it was our only comrade, our one trusted confidant. So it joined us, Death did, on this journey across the seas and carried us away whenever our spirits surrendered. Many learned to lay their lives, without illness or accident, into Death's hands. They simply bowed their heads and died. We'd never seen such a thing. Even Death was surprised. However, those of us whom Death skipped over, the unfortunate ones, we lived—and each day we lived, we etched grooves into the planks upon which we lay, counting our days at sea.

The evening and the morning were the first day.

. . .

The next day, we woke to shouts and curses from captors,

commanding us to open our mouths for daily victuals. Most did not hesitate. Our hunger had not been satisfied since we'd left our villages. Their food was strange and distasteful, yet we swallowed it still, hoping only to survive. Its taste revealed its contents: beans, flour, cornmeal, water. Mere mush. Some vomited as soon as it was received. Some swallowed just enough to stay alive. Some wouldn't take it at all. Starvation was their weapon, and they fought valiantly. A few spat mush back into captors' faces. They were killed on the spot. And that's precisely what they'd wanted—immediate death that gave no joy to the murderer. As for the rest of us, we swallowed what we could and prayed that, wherever we were going, it would be a land of plenty. If we'd known then what we know now, all of us might've refused food and succumbed to Death's invitation. But we didn't know.

The remainder of the day we lay in abject misery. Tossed to and fro, our backs were rubbed raw. The slightest movement caused immeasurable pain. Many suffered sickness of motion. Some went out of their minds. Some began to hate themselves for being unable to fight. For having given traders the benefit of the doubt. For having ignored the signs of communal distress. For having killed men from other villages who were now family. Many shouted curses at a God who would allow such a calamity. They resolved to rid the world, one day, of the enemy, if they ever got free. Others lay motionless, no doubt staring, in their minds, at memories of home. Still others wailed. We wailed the names of our women above, whose screeches and pleadings drove us mad. We wailed for those who'd be dead by morning. We wailed for sons without fathers. Fathers without families. Families without communities. Communities without elders. Elders without children. We wailed from stench so horrendous it made us sick. We wailed to remind ourselves we still existed. Mostly we wailed because we didn't know what else to do. A few struggled in their chains until wrists and ankles were worn, bloody, white flesh. Many squeezed their eyes shut, hoping against hope that this was all a bad dream. It was not.

The evening and the morning were the second day.

. . .

Each morning, they dragged us to our feet, still bound inches apart, and took us above deck. Coming out of darkness, the sunlight blinded. The ship swayed. We leaned upon one another to keep from falling over. Soon our eyes adjusted and we looked around. The land had disappeared. Which way was home?

A young boy, whom we'd never seen, beat a makeshift drum, and captors beat us until we danced. Chains sliced our flesh with each movement, but we had no choice. Furious blood streaked the upper deck of the ship, leaving it slippery and stained deep red. Still, we danced. We danced the dances we knew. We danced Kuku and Manjani, Sorsonet and Soli. We tried to explain that what we were doing was against our beliefs, that our dances were sacred and not to be performed unless in the context of ritual, but they did not understand our words. It wouldn't have mattered anyway.

Several danced a new dance toward the ship's edge where they, burdened with heavy irons, plunged into the Great Mother, pulling with them the willing and unwilling. Their bodies sank instantly out of sight. We watched water swirl where they disappeared. After several days of this new dance, captors made nets that rested beneath the boat and rose instantly when people thought they were free, restoring their bodies to the boat. The recovered were confined to the lower decks where they lay like zombies, unconnected to life's flow. They were never stable again. Not in their minds. We pitied them more than ourselves. They were already dead.

Big fish awaited our flesh. After tasting our blood, they moved in harmony with the ship, ready at any moment to feed. We wondered if they tasted, in the bodies they consumed, our rage and fury. If they knew they were consuming fire and wrath. If they knew they were now the carriers of human anger and madness. If they knew that the very waters of their living were now saturated with willing and unwilling souls. Of course they didn't. They couldn't have known that we, the proud people of the black land, would become their major source of sustenance. They couldn't have known that, for the next two hundred years, they'd chase slave ships until, long after the trade, they'd swim the triangular route still, looking for rations they could not find. They couldn't have known that slowly, year by year, the ocean's water would ingest a people's fury so completely that hurricanes would come each season and claim lives in recompense for Africans gone overboard. They couldn't have known that, of the people eaten, some would've healed the world. Some would've traveled galaxies and discovered life in other forms. Some would've healed cancers and diseases unnamed. Some would've founded institutions that teach people how to see God. Some would've found ways to restore a lost, troubled mind. Some would've walked the planet loving the unlovable. Some would've learned the language of animals and intercepted their ways. Some would've discovered, while yet living, the dimensions of the afterlife. Some would've uncovered the secret of time travel, which our people had contemplated for centuries. Some would've gone to the bottom of the ocean and retrieved African bones that had been discarded carelessly, and buried them the way a human ought to be buried. And some would've spent their lives mourning for a world that spoke constantly of a God but clearly never knew one. We lay in the belly of the ship, trying to imagine their lives in the invisible. Our minds could not see that far. So, instead, we prayed that, in death, they were returned home and that their spirits danced a dance of a new dawn.

The evening and the morning were the sixth day.

• • •

On day seven a young man's calm, silent disposition captured our attention. He studied our weary eyes, then nodded slowly as if knowing something we didn't. Distress and trauma had not broken him; he shared our rage, as any man would, but something else occupied his mind. Something deep in the soul that could not be spoken. Something the oppressors could not disturb or destroy. Something unnamable, immeasurable, indestructible. We could not discern his preoccupation, but we saw the empty space in his eyes. This was not his reality. He was here, but he was not here. Whenever we looked at him, he looked through us—staring, it seemed, at something so beautiful, so magical, his gaze could not be broken. Some spoke his language, but he would not answer their inquiries. However, there was no hatred in his silence; only clarity in his eyes revealing that he would never, ever be another man's captive. Those who knew him called him Abuto, which means "the secrets of the heart are hidden deep within."

The following morning, we discovered the source of his fixation. Standing upon the upper deck, waiting to be danced, Abuto trembled as his eyes met those of a woman. They said nothing, made no gesture of recognition, but their eyes bore desire and hope too strong to be concealed. We nodded. We saw it—the dance of love in their eyes—and as we danced, their spirits danced another dance and even our dance was for them. Had the captors known, they surely would've tried to break this bond, to strip these lovers of the last vestige of joy they knew, so we tried not to look at them or they at each other. Yet the tug of love pulled nonetheless, and occasionally their eyes met and brightened. We tried to distract the captors' attention away from them that they might get a few precious moments of seeing and perhaps even brush each other's flesh. That alone would have to be enough. At least for now. And it was. It was comforting to see these captive lovebirds refusing to deny the only thing they knew for sure.

When we descended the stairs and returned to our planks of pain, Abuto stared into nothingness as tears marked his cheekbones. These were not tears of sadness. No, he wept from knowing that the keeper of his heart still existed above. He wept because she had not given up and jumped overboard. He wept because he had left home in love and the feeling had never subsided. He wept because, in the midst of insanity and trauma, he had not lost love. Through them, we realized that, though bound and suffering, we possessed something that could never be taken away. We'd known it from the beginning. Elders had told of love's elusive nature, how it lurks in the hearts of people and surfaces uninvited. They'd taught us that love could never be conquered or possessed. It must simply be enjoyed. And when two find it, their spirits mesh into one. Love comes that there might be life. We'd spent our childhoods waiting to be in love, to know, finally, the magical feeling people get when they discover their soul's compliment, and now we saw that it could never be destroyed. Abuto and the woman upstairs reminded us that no power on earth could extract love from a person's heart. We thanked God for the reminder. Our breathing eased.

And then came the storm.

It lasted three days. It tossed the boat right and left, back and forth, with no regard for its human cargo. Voices screamed and shouted, from fear and immutable pain. Only the chains held us secure. Vomit covered the ship floor. More died, including some of the crewmen above. With each passing hour, we were less and less sure any of us would survive.

When the storm calmed, diseases crept in among us. We had no cure for such strange maladies. Perhaps if we'd been home we could've boiled leaves, tree bark, or roots to ward off these deadly illnesses but, as it were, we had no defenses against the invisible predators whose single joy was our total obliteration. Their names were scurvy, dysentery, or what they called the flux. Each had its own specialty, its own commitment to our destruction, and each performed courageously. In their presence, many could not hold their stool. Bowels moved without permission, leaving people streaked with runny fecal matter and bloody pus. Others could hold no food, regardless of their consumption. Their throats, tender from constant regurgitation, shed blood as if scourging the lining of the esophagus. A few shook from nervous systems gone awry. Their entire bodies trembled and never settled. Wrist and ankle shackles, like beaded shekeres, beat out sixteenth rhythms against the wood on which they lay. It was a symphony of suffering and death, a melody of sorrow and grief, captured by those whose one desire was to escape bondage and enter a realm of everlasting peace. We could only listen to the song. We could not sing it. There were no words. Just blurred rhythms driven by human anguish and torment.

When the rhythms slowed into whole notes, we knew the end was near. And when Death came, we called our comrades' names or a name that could've been theirs, as a verbal libation and communal recognition of a friend, a brother, a baba, an *umi* who had begun the journey with us but would not see the end. We slept next to Death until bodies were tossed overboard to the giant fish that awaited. These were our loved ones, our sisters and brothers. Gone but not forgotten.

In his nightmare, Abuto screamed, "Chisanganda!" His head tossed and his chains rattled. Someone touched him and when he woke, he shivered with unspeakable dread. We did not know the content of his vision, but whatever it was, it left him frightened enough to scream even louder: *"Chisanganda! Chisanganda!"* We tried to quiet him, to avoid a visitation from crewmen above, but he would not be consoled. Only light tapping from the upper deck, like the rhythm of a song, confirmed that she'd heard him and so his fretting ceased. But he continued to murmur her name throughout the night, as if conjuring some sort of protective shield around her.

During dance the next morning, Abuto stared at all of us, even his lover, with fear and sadness. He'd seen something in the night, something troubling, something disturbing. He didn't seem to believe the way he once had.

She felt his misgiving and wore a frown of disapproval. But the problem dwelled in his head—not his heart. He loved her no less than the day before, but he'd seen, in his dream, his lover violated. He saw her reaching for him, but they could not connect. Captors dragged her away as others held him at bay. This he relayed to the few who shared his tongue. It was a bad omen, they said. Spirits had sent him a warning. Some tried to say that dreams are not to be taken literally, but they didn't believe that. Abuto didn't either. They'd come from people who trusted dreams as much as they trusted God. So, yes, something would happen, and he'd be unable to protect her, and he couldn't live with that. Not now. Not ever. She was everything to him, everything he had. We shook our heads and prayed silently. Abuto sighed. It was only a matter of time.

With anxious energy, we began to create rhythms with our fists and feet. All of us. On one accord. Together. One person would introduce a beat, and the rest of us would add our complimentary thump until the entire lower portion of the ship shook. *Thump, thump, thump* joined *thump, de-dump, de-dump, dump,* which then joined *dat-dat-dat-dat-dat-dat,* which then joined *dat-dat-dat, bump, bump, dat-dat-dat, bump, bump,* which then joined *bump, bump . . .* (rest) *. . . bump bump . . .* (rest), which then joined loud bangs of 4-count whole

notes: *BOOOOOOM! BOOOOOOM! BOOOOOOM!*
The sound was so intimidating they dared not try to stop
it. If they'd killed us all, that would've been a blessing.
And a deep financial loss. So we beat rhythms for hours.
Loudly. Softly. Angrily. Sometimes we did it in unison,
creating a stronger, more direct sound. Sometimes we
swayed our heads to the beat. Sometimes our teeth chattered along. Sometimes we cried. Most times we didn't.
Sometimes we lay exhausted afterward, feeling good that
we'd made ourselves known. Sometimes we beat our
own traditional rhythms. Sometimes we played along
with the sea. Sometimes our ancestors joined in and
played djembes and djun djuns right next to us. Then, as
the rhythms waned, they faded into the atmosphere.

The evening and the morning were the thirteenth day.

. . .

Our humming began at a cool, even pace, when beats
were slow and lulling. A man purred a dark melody, then
repeated it. It wasn't a groan from pain and desolation,
but deliberate lines of constructed meter and time that
jarred our spirits and invited our participation. One by
one, we joined in—some in upper registers, some in the
depths of our voices—having found a language that
needed no words. We hummed until we knew we'd sur-

vive. We hummed until we released mothers and fathers whom we'd never see again. We hummed until our love for and gratitude to each other was clear. We hummed a celebration for living. For fighting. For refusing to die. For enduring when giving up would've been easier. For still believing, against all odds, that we'd get home some-day. We hummed our commitment to raise children, wherever we went, in the way of our people. We hummed that our women, slightly above, might know we hadn't forgotten them. We hummed for the dead lying next to us. We hummed for children not yet born. We hummed for children born, but left behind. We hummed for kins-men, yesterday's enemies, who were now precious, cov-eted friends.

Sometimes we hummed to mute the screeching and pleading of our young women. They were girls, some of them, barely thirteen or fourteen rains, screaming from their very souls. The echo never settled. It rang through-out the hull, disrupting our sleep. Our only defense was to hum, so we hummed that they might know we were with them. That they might be reminded that captors could mar their bodies but not their spirits. That they might know his forced entry did not disturb their beauty. That they might know the day would come when we'd loose our chains and stand guard over their virtue. But until then we believed that, as long as we hummed, the timbre of our voices would keep them.

Occasionally, young men, too, were thus violated. They fought like cornered lions. It always took three or four crewmen to subdue one of our boys. Then, with his strength exhausted and pride wounded, he was dragged up the wooden stairs to the place of defilement. We heard his screaming each step of the way. It was a hollow kind of roar, housed in a deep, innocent place. We saw, in our minds, his mouth stretched wide and eyes bulging. When he returned, his face was a blank stare. They threw him, like a corpse, into his holding place and, once again, bound him with chains. We begged him not to surrender, but our words, we feared, were useless babbling. So we hummed some more until slowly, painfully, he cried and joined the chorus of protection for himself or another who screamed, wept, moaned, fought, and was still overcome in battle. Then we sighed.

The evening and the morning were the fifteenth day.

. . .

Sometimes they bled profusely. It was a peculiar odor, the smell of sexual violation, a mixture of rotting flesh and underarm stench. They shivered even though the heat belowdecks would've suffocated the weak. Our desecrated brothers survived because, as best we could, we reminded them of who they were. Still, most were never the same again. Some never spoke another word. Some never married. Some couldn't look at a woman again, even their own mothers and sisters. Some wanted to touch and hold lovers, but their arms could not embrace. Some conceived thoughts too vile and heinous to repeat. Most considered their own destruction. One tender, beautiful brother, smothered with the captor's stench, dashed his head against his plank until we were sure his brains would spill onto the floor. An older man turned and whispered something in his ear, restoring his life. The young man did not understand his elder's words, but he heard his heart, and he survived. Most were not so fortunate.

We needed our gatekeepers. Those who traversed the boundaries of sexuality and spirit, those whose hearts and bodies knew no limitations. They could've told us how to heal rape from within. They would've reassured us that unless a body invites another's entry, the memory cannot linger. Yes, the sting would never be forgotten, but it need not govern one's consciousness. Simply from their touch we could've been reminded that to expunge a person from our spirit is to erase them from our hearts. We'd been taught this. Yet in the midst of trauma, re-membering is difficult. Our gatekeepers stood at the edge of our village, watching and studying the world, prepared to protect us from any potential invasion. They had more eyes than the rest of us. They knew freedom in ways we did not. They loved each other, men or women, without public ridicule. They were free to express themselves without boundaries or restrictions. We loved them. In their presence, we prospered.

Yet without them, unable to see our future, we took refuge in memory. Endless hours were spent reconstructing lives far more perfect than we'd actually lived. We saw in our minds thatched huts and compounds, shaded by trees on every side. We heard children running from playmates and teasing each other about whom they liked. We saw elders sitting and drinking wine from kola nuts, wondering about the future of our people. We heard men speak of the difficulty of living with women. We heard women speak of their frustrations with men. We saw hunters sharpening arrows in preparation for the hunt. We saw weavers laughing together as they assembled ,multicolored cloth, which, one day, would be our pride and glory. We saw farmers' sweat drip from their chins as they tilled the soil. We saw women braid dried grass until they'd made intricate carrying baskets. We saw the sun set across the plains and leave streaks of purple and gold in the sky. Then we saw fires built for night rituals, which aimed to cleanse the community of bad spirits. We saw ancestors stand watch over those whom they honored. And of course we heard the drums. Everyone. Everywhere. In every village. They beat with the regularity of the heart itself. Deep rhythms reverberated across the plains, through trees, and into the heavens. It was the language of our gods, the collective voice of a people. The drum's polyrhythmic repertoire surpassed the number of hairs on our heads. Even on rainy days, it rumbled praises, far in the distance, to the Great God who'd sent nourishment to the earth. It also admonished and celebrated us. One studied many years before mastering the drum. Most never played it, but we understood its message loud and clear. In the bottom of the ship, we heard it, too, ringing in our memories.

This made our past perfect. We conjured images of loving parents although everyone had not had them. We imagined walking in forests with sages and soothsayers whom we couldn't possibly have known. We played, in our minds, with siblings never born. We ate juicy fruits beneath groves of verdant trees, most of which actually bore minimally. We lay our dead to rest without grief. We prayed to God, and God answered us. We lived in harmony with wild animals. Elders were always wise and upstanding in character. Of course we knew better. But in exile we chose to remember the best of what we'd had. Or to create it. All of us recalled a people too strong to be overtaken. But, of course, that couldn't have been true.

When storms came again, memories faded. Reality returned. Sometimes it rained for days, as wind and waves pounded the ship's hull. Blasts of fury threatened to dismantle the vessel and set the captives free. If only we'd been so blessed. Our stomachs turned constantly and bile dribbled from the corners of our mouths. Tears streaked our cheeks without our ability to wipe them. Some screamed through their anguish. Others squeezed their eyes and endured. We'd had slaves, too, but only in recompense for debts owed or as prisoners of war. And even then they were never publically disgraced. Not like this. Regardless of their crime, we would not have been allowed to bind and beat them and take them so far away they could never get home. It simply wasn't our way.

We wondered now why we had ever fought each other. What had made us think we were enemies? We believed basically the same things! That there was one God. That the land was ours collectively. That family is the core of any strong community. How had we taken each other's lives so easily? There was something we claimed to believe about the sanctity of life that we had not practiced. We wanted to apologize to each other, but there were no words. Only regret. We wanted to bow before each other in humble correction, but we could not. We were all guilty. Perhaps our bondage was recompense for having spilt each other's blood. Silence shielded our shame, our remorse, our admission that we were, at least in part, architects of our own situation. We knew it. All of us. We'd been warriors at each other's expense. We'd gained wealth from what we'd taken. And now we all had to pay.

The evening and the morning were the nineteenth day.

. . .

Captors visited our compartment every evening, though not for very long. When they arrived, the stench drove them away in seconds. It was thick and heavy like smoke, permeating their pores and leaving a bad taste on their tongues. As for us, we spit constantly, sometimes on ourselves, sometimes on each other, sometimes on the floor, trying desperately to keep the putrid taste out of our mouths. Still it lingered. For some, it never went away. Every time they chewed or swallowed, they tasted the flavor of bondage. They were nauseous for a lifetime.

Sadness evolved into resistance. We were unwilling to surrender, no matter how bleak. We were angry, mostly with ourselves, but we had not lost the will to fight. We simply couldn't understand why this lesson had come. Yet we determined to survive it.

Our greatest hurdle was language. We were from the same land, but many spoke very different tongues. After some weeks, though, we began to speak with our hands and eyes, creating a basic system of communication all of us understood. Sometimes we banged on wood to get others' attention. Sometimes we bulged our eyes to say *Don't give up*. Sometimes we growled and grunted so our anger would not consume us. Sometimes we beat our heads against bed planks and, when others joined in, we knew we were becoming unified. Sometimes we even tried to smile, but our pain was often too much to bear. So we hid our hearts behind rhythms and melodies that spoke what the mouth could not.

This way, we planned our mutiny. A great warrior from the village of Kuntaur rattled his chains one afternoon, after we had danced and been returned belowdecks. He seemed frantic but not insane, so we yielded our attention. His eyes opened so large we thought they'd pop from his head. We quickly discerned that he had an escape plan. He motioned, with his head, to various individuals, and we nodded. When his head rolled in a circle, we knew he was instructing all of us. To some he gave the task of fighting. To others the job of gathering weapons. To the Mende, the charge of watching and paying attention, since they were known as people with three eyes. To several others the responsibility of protecting women and children. To some the mission of gathering ancestral support. To others the duty of steering the ship—if we got free. Somehow we comprehended his delegation.

Days passed in silence. We dreamed of killing captors. Of fighting like warriors and hunters determined to destroy our enemy. Of swimming home and telling our story. Of being reunited with loved ones and standing as family again. We imagined big fish tasting a different flesh this time. We thought how proud our gods would be that we rose up and proclaimed our liberty. At whatever cost. We dreamed of chains broken and discarded. Guns aimed at sea-blue eyes. Free black souls standing at the ship's edge, staring into the water, remembering those who could not wait for freedom.

On the twenty-third or twenty-fourth day, another storm arose while we danced. Dark clouds gathered and shifted in the heavens, leaving us anxious and fretful. Wind gushed and whispered in our ears. Waves dashed against the boat, as if trying to get our attention. We looked at the warrior. He nodded repeatedly. It was time.

Our women, those without shackles, led the revolt. How they knew the plan we did not know, but we were grateful. And they were fierce in battle. They attacked captors like starving lionesses, gouging eyes and ripping flesh with bare teeth. More pale enemies intervened, but they, too, were made to bear the marks of our women's rage. Sisters, mothers, and daughters fought with the strength and fortitude of elephants. We cheered them on. One woman secured the key for our chains and began to set us free. She was shot and killed within seconds. Some called her Abeni, which means, "We asked for her, and behold, we got her." We promised, in our hearts, to add her name to the list of African heroes before whom we bowed.

Several men were now unbound and added their power to the destruction of pale faces. Never did crewmen imagine we could reach into chests and extract hearts with our bare hands. They didn't know we could end their breathing with one blow to the throat. Surprise leapt in their eyes. Our strength multiplied. One of our boys assumed the key to our chains and continued what Abeni had begun. Within seconds he, too, entered the ancestral realm. We would call their names at future ceremonies. We would pour libations to their priceless memory. We would name our sons and daughters after them. But, for now, with more men loosed, we fought on.

The spilling of captors' blood fueled our efforts. Those assigned to weapons found them and distributed guns, machetes, and sticks with which we destroyed one pale crewman after another. When the lad with the key fell, an enemy confiscated it, leaving half our men bound. Yet, even in that state, we fought. Some wrapped their chains around enemy necks and pulled until air ceased flowing. A few slammed steel shackles against pale foreheads. All shouted names of gods and ancestors whose help we so desperately needed. *Allah, won't you come? Yemaya, give us strength! Baba Kwesi, where are you? Ogun, show your mighty power! Shango, set your people free!* For a moment, a precious fleeting moment, we were delivered.

Then more pale faces appeared. They seemed to materialize from the very floor of the ship. They pointed guns at our heads and hearts. The battle was over. The deck of the ship was covered with bodies of our comrades, some only half dead. The warrior lay among them, pride beaming from his eyes. We, the living, were hurried belowdecks and chained once again.

With a strap called a cat-o'-nine-tails, we were beaten for our insurgence. Blood covered our backs. Humiliation covered our spirits. When angry captors left, silence lingered. We didn't look at one another or say a word. We didn't hum, we didn't moan. We didn't grunt, we didn't shout. We didn't even move. We simply lay there, staring at planks above and beside us, promising that, one day, we'd try again.

In the weeks that followed, we thought of other ways to resist. Starvation was the common choice. Many simply clamped their mouths shut. Crewmen used an instrument called a "speculum" to pry them open and shove food down their throats as if they were insubordinate beasts of the field. They often gagged and gave it back. Sometimes they lost their lives. Other times, they simply starved.

Just as before, some decided to die. We'd heard from our sages of the power of the mind over the body. It was an issue of consciousness, they'd said, of one's mastery of the Will. So, one or two simply closed their eyes and willingly took Death's hand. It was a kind of melancholy of the soul, a choice to exit the flesh and dwell forever in the spirit. Only the most mature among us could do it. The rest had not reached that level of initiation. Captors frowned at perfectly healthy bodies suddenly devoid of life. They didn't know what we knew. They didn't know who we were.

Our people had studied such things for centuries. Priests and sages spent years mastering universal knowledge, learning the secrets of the cosmos. Day and night they searched to understand the relationship between the earth and the moon, the sun and the human heart. They kept records of the coming and going of seasons that we might plant with precision and harvest with abundance. They taught the importance of living in harmony with the earth's rhythm. Pregnancies were monitored by the rotations of the moon, deliveries made easier with the assistance of the earth's pull. We caught rain from our thatched rooftops and thus were rarely desperate for drinking water. Some discovered ways to subject their will to the will of God. They were the ones who died without captors' assistance. They stepped into the everlasting simply because they chose to.

Each day our numbers dwindled. At the start, there was hardly room in our compartment to breathe. Now, empty spaces hovered. We were lonely for kinsmen gone overboard. In those shackled hours, we'd connected with unknown neighbors and fought for freedom alongside those who had once been enemies. On the ship, we didn't care who governed the eastern corner of the forest. We didn't care if a young man had ten cows for a bride price or none at all. We didn't care how low one chief bowed before another. We didn't care if our necklaces and other adornment looked too much like our neighbors'. We didn't care that someone had stepped onto our territory without permission from the council. We didn't care that some believed in a *chi,* or personal god, and some didn't. We didn't care that someone owed us for the slaying of a lion outside the legal boundary. And we certainly didn't care that some had riches while others had none. Facing an enemy more formidable than any we'd ever known, all we cared about was surviving. Together.

The evening and the morning were the fortieth day.

• • •

Whenever the sea calmed, we pondered our fate. Where were we going? To the land of our captors? Would we survive there? Did they plan to eat us? Some stared at others who spoke their tongue, but few said anything. We thought about the chaos in our villages that the raids had left behind. We thought about the reaping of crops we'd worked so hard to plant. We thought about young siblings who'd never be initiated. We thought about what it meant to be a man. We thought about the travails of our women. We thought about the joy of courtship rituals. We thought about *fufu* and *kankan* and stewed goat. We thought about our unclothed bodies, used for filthy pleasures and nighttime warming. We thought about whether our children would ever honor us again. We thought about ways to make recompense with our gods. We thought about how to tell the story of our bondage to future generations. We thought about learning captors' language in order to know what they said about us. And we thought about how pale crewmen became so cruel.

With each body tossed into the mouth of the Great Mother, we drifted further from our homeland, our traditions, our people, and closer to a world we knew nothing about. Forsaking hope of ever seeing home again, some of our kinsmen committed crimes against themselves that made us shudder. One man ripped open his throat with his fingernails. Blood gathered upon the plank beneath him, then dripped to the floor in streams of red. He sighed and relaxed until all life escaped him. We called him Jabulani, which means "His smile lights the path." Another man hummed a dark melody as he slammed his head against a wooden beam in the center of the ship. He repeated this behavior throughout the night. By morning, his humming had ceased and his head hung limp over the edge of the plank. He was a young man, no more than twenty rains. We called him Idirisi, which means "He is dedicated." Two women, perhaps mother and daughter, sat in a corner facing each other. Somehow they had secured small knives, undoubtedly from the cabin wherein they'd been assaulted, and now, with the force of a hyena's jaws, buried those blades simultaneously in each other's bellies. Besides a slight moan, they made no sound. They collapsed in each other's arms and walked into the spirit realm together. Captor's kicked and cursed when they found them, bemoaning the money they'd lose, yet their only choice was to feed them to the sea. We nodded as they dragged them away. We called them Andaiye and Adinike, which means "She strives to know herself" and "This one comes but once in a life-time.".

Crewmen came belowdecks one day, a few moons after the uprising, and beat us again with instruments we'd never seen. We'd been flailed with cat-o'-nine-tails and sticks, but these were larger whips that tore our flesh asunder. The pain was unimaginable. Throughout the hull, the smell and sound of ripping flesh loitered for days. Flies gathered to lick our open wounds. We tried to shoo them away, but they persisted until crewmen, understanding apparently the potential cost of such mutilation, returned and covered our sores with thick ointment. Soon blisters scabbed over and peeled away. We never figured out why they beat us so that day. All we knew was that they meant to claim us as their own. Someone had bought us and they meant to own us forever.

Yet if we'd been bought, we reasoned, we must've been sold. But by whom? Who'd had the power to do such a thing? Truth was, there were many. In separate tongues, several were considered such as Ayokunle of the Yoruba. He was one of the chief's men who owned more cattle than most. Perhaps he'd traded our flesh for more grazing territory. Or maybe it had been Ikenna of the Ibo. He was a weaver who hardly spoke a word. People whispered of his unpredictable nature and his questionable integrity. Yes, it could've been him. Or perhaps it had been Kwaku of the Akan who sold some of us away. Deceit and stealth shrouded his character, his people agreed. Parents warned children to avoid his cunning nature and not to envy his excessive. Kave, too, of the Wolof had proven untrustworthy, some remembered, having been accused, though never convicted, of several offenses due to his lying tongue. We considered practically everyone who held any position of authority. Yet there was simply no way to know. Would our own kinsmen have traded our flesh for trinkets of silver and gold? Would chiefs have justified our bondage in exchange for silk and salt? The more we pondered, the more convinced we became that someone in our own villages had participated in our capture. It simply couldn't have happened otherwise. Captors didn't know enough about us to destroy us so easily. They couldn't have subdued hundreds of warriors unless they knew where they would be prior to the attack. Someone must've told them. It was the only explanation. And when we went to retrieve weapons, they were not there. Captors could not have found our weapons on their own. They were hidden in a secret place for just such an ambush as this. Someone must've told them! As we thought about it, even the time of the attacks appeared calculated. Our strength was divided. Elders were in council meetings, warriors were combing the forest, other adults were tending gardens. Young children were consumed with play, older children were being initiated. We were living our simple, though multifaceted, lives. It was the perfect time for an onslaught. That's how we knew someone must have assisted from the inside. The timing was simply too deliberate. The destruction was too complete. We hung our heads and sighed.

It could've been some powerful women, too. Several held positions of authority without reputations of excellence. Like Fortee of the Bassa. She loved nothing like she loved riches. Elders whispered that she'd married her husband only because he'd had countless cows and goats and barns of yams. Her arms were always covered with gold bangles, and, even outside of rituals, rare stones hung from her neck. Her vanity could not be disguised. Many resented her. But could she have loved those things more than us? We didn't know.

Perhaps it had been the one they called Kadiatou of the Fulani. She had been found suspect in her people's hearts. Her attitude stank like rotten fish. She could've done it. She didn't like anyone. No man ever sought her company. It was sad, really, being so young *and* bitter. No one knew what caused it, but everyone saw it. She cursed the world with her sarcasm and scorn. It could've been her. It could've been anyone. It was definitely someone. Small wonder our gods wouldn't save us. We hadn't saved each other.

The evening and the morning were the forty-sixth

day.

. . .

Over time, we trained ourselves to forget. Survival was easier that way. We remembered *truths*, certainly, but facts were dispensable. Like the fact that more of us died than survived on this journey. Or the fact that we didn't let the land rest every seven years as we were supposed to. Or the fact that some of our men married girls before they were mature in their bodies. Or the fact that some of our chiefs had been chosen not for their integrity, but for their beauty. Or the fact that some children were exempted from communal duties because of who their parents were. Or the fact that some women—men, too!—spent more time adorning themselves than rearing their children. We simply let details dissolve into the atmosphere as the ship rocked to and fro.

We forgot many other things, too. There was no room in our hearts for newfound sorrows. Most of our tears had been shed. Every distress we experienced was a distress from the day before. The human heart has limitations, we discovered, which we reached long before our voyage was over. But we had not given up. We *could* not. We simply wanted to live. We knew how to die. That had been proven. Now we wanted to live. For those who had died and who'd been forced to die. For those back in the motherland who had taught us the value of life. For children we would birth in a new world. For ancestors who let us get our lesson but loved us still. For those who lay beside us for weeks—raped, maimed, dehumanized, belittled, insulted—we wanted to live! To speak the truth, one day, about a people too strong to be destroyed completely. To tell the world how we'd survived what no human should've survived. To sing songs that reminded us forever of the price we'd paid to exist. To create new dances that explain far more than the tongue can say. To sculpt images—dark, beautiful, black, sacred images—of warriors, prophets, and healers whose blood aligned in the bellies of those slave ships and became one blood. To paint canvases of stoic men and women standing together with little but themselves and their children, and making that enough. We were tired of dying. We wanted to live!

The evening and the morning were the fiftieth day.

· · ·

Their food still made us nauseated, but more of us ate it. They beat us anyway, just as before, but we learned to ignore the pain. The ship's rocking still bruised our already-bruised flesh, but we moaned less now. The shrieks and cries of women and men being entered without permission still chilled our blood, but we saved our breath for another day. When their medicine man made his rounds to see if their diseases had consumed us, we stared at him, leaving him more frightened than ever. When they took us above deck for dancing, we moved without provocation. They thought they'd won. They believed they'd finally achieved our submission. They were wrong.

Truth was, we were more dangerous than before. People determined to survive are willing to sacrifice anything to achieve that end. Captors sensed a shift in our energy and became watchful. They were wise to do so. Instead of once or twice a day, they now visited our quarters hourly, seeking the nature and purpose of our newfound poise. They poked us with the butts of their rifles, but we responded like dead men. A few studied our faces, but met only solid resolve to destroy them one day. They concluded that, just as before, we must be planning an uprising. So they determined to dissuade us.

The next day, immediately after dancing, we were instructed to remain on deck. Crewmen had their guns drawn and pointed at us from every direction. Unable to understand their tongue, we studied their gestures and discerned that our suspicions had been right—they suspected us of planning another mutiny. They grabbed one of our sisters—no one knew her name—and bound her with thick ropes. They lifted her, screaming the while, with the mast of the sail, and slowly lowered her body into the water. When they lifted her again, her lower half was gone. Some monster of the sea had taken it. Shreds of ragged flesh dangled from her bloody midsection. Within seconds, she was dead. Most of us turned away. It was a sight unfit for human eyes. A few tried to comprehend what kind of people these captors were, but there was no comprehension.

They lowered the rest of her into the water and let the monsters complete their feasting. We closed our eyes and trembled. Our prayer was that she entered the next world whole. Then they took an African lad, a boy of no more than ten rains, and doused him with oil. We told him, with our eyes, of a magical world where he was going, a place where there'd be no more suffering. He nodded and smiled. Then a crewman set him ablaze. For a moment, he ran in circles, shrieking words in his own tongue as the fire consumed him. Then he collapsed to the floor of the deck. Most of us cried aloud and covered our eyes. A few beheld the boy's demise in its entirety. They saw his spirit ascend into the cloudless blue sky as his flesh turned black beneath the flames. Someone said his name was Toundi, which means "Our abounding joy."

Days passed in mumbled rage: *Didn't these men know better? Wouldn't they stand before the judgment? Isn't there one righteous man among them? Where are their mothers? And what of their fathers? Yes! These seasoned men of valor and pride. Where are they? Or their fathers' elders. They must have elders. And when do they do their rituals? In their cabins at night? But rituals cannot be done alone! Perhaps they live only in one realm. Yes, there's the answer! They have only two eyes and as such cannot see how this realm prepares them for the next. And that realm for the next. And so on.* But still if we had listened to the old prophets, we would've seen these pale people coming before they came. In the end, we cursed ourselves alone.

The evening and the morning were the fifty-fourth day.

. . .

The nauseating stench never went away. It loitered in the air like smoke. It was the smell of feces, musty bodies, and death. It was a peculiar odor, unlike anything we'd ever known. It violated our nostrils, causing nose hairs to tingle. It was a heavy odor that lingered in our throats and stifled our breathing. We never forgot it. Often, when taken above deck for dancing, we gave thanks for clean, salty air. Then, descending the staircase, we were once again overcome by the pungent, sickening scent. Our bellies rumbled. At times they tried to cleanse the hold with buckets of seawater, but that only increased the moisture in an already damp, musty space. Defecation, puke, spoiled food, urine, menstrual blood, pus, mucus from open sores, and mounds of spittle combined to create a half-inch gravy that covered the ship floor. It was a haven for diseases, waiting to multiply and devour us. A crewman appeared one day with a broom, and after two strokes shook his head and left. He tried to clamp his nose with one hand and manipulate the broomstick with the other, but it was impossible. As for us, we learned to breathe less often and to spit when particles gathered on our tongues.

Some of the stench was our hatred for pale flesh. Malice has an odor, we knew, like that of musty armpits. We'd smelled it before. Now it wafted through the air as we dreamed, day after day, of mutilating captors. One man's teeth chattered whenever crewmen approached. Words of fury burbled from his lips, explaining how he envisioned dismembering these people, one arm, one leg, one foot at a time. Another man announced, in the silence of midnight, that if he ever got free, he would sacrifice his life to bury a machete in the hearts of as many crewmen as possible. He'd lost the hope for laughing children and magenta sunsets; all he desired was the slaughter of those who'd slaughtered us. He wanted to make them pay for thinking we weren't men. For ruining homes and villages they had not built. For separating us from people we'd always known. For leaving children to rebuild villages without instructions. And for taking us so far away we could never return. We listened and nodded.

Our women also dreamed of slicing captors into tiny pieces and tossing them into the sea. They said this while we danced. They imagined scratching gray and green eyeballs until they dripped red with blood. They imagined burying knives and twisting them in pale stomachs and throats. One of our sisters lost her life after marring a crewman with her lioness claws. Rivers of blood, like our warrior marks, streaked his face. He was hardly recognizable. They threw her overboard, alive, as she screamed "Ashe! Ashe!" We wondered what our women, in a new land, would teach girls about men. We dared not guess.

The evening and the morning were the fifty-sixth day.

· · ·

In the midst of inconceivable rage and guilt, a young man reminded us once again that we, too, had had slaves. That was no secret, we said. But we'd never held them captive to our own spirits. When they paid their debts, they were incorporated into our communities or returned to their villages. Some married our daughters and sons. Some became representative members of our councils. Some trained in our healing arts. Some smoked pipes and drank palm wine with our elders. Some became sages whose wisdom we followed. None were stabbed in the eye. Or raped savagely. Or set ablaze. Or fed, piece by piece, to ravenous beasts of the sea. Our gods wouldn't have been pleased. The young man sighed heavily and nodded. We'd heard of people from the north, followers of Allah, who'd come centuries before and razed our villages. They, too, took away slaves and brutalized them. But these were not our people. We were certainly imperfect, but we respected life. At least we were taught to.

We needed our elders now. They would know what to say. Captors had been shrewd in leaving them behind. They must've known that people devoid of elders are a conquered people. Truth was, in spiritual terms, we were children. A few knew some of our people's secrets, but most had not completed those levels of initiation. So our normal ascent into maturity and spiritual understanding ceased. It simply leveled out. We came from people who believed that spirituality was a journey one took consciously, and if one sought the upper levels of God, one could know the workings of invisible things. We believed in the ability to transcend the physical world. We knew that spirit was more potent than flesh. This knowledge was barely the beginning of our spiritual consciousness.

We'd been taught, all of us, in various ways and to various degrees, that the spirit of a person is everlasting. It's the body that is temporal. However, in the hull of the ship, it was practically impossible to maintain spiritual clarity while we were being mutilated. Deeper levels of knowing and higher realms of consciousness devolved into theories that seemed to have no application. We couldn't separate our condition from our convictions. Most had not achieved that mastery.

So we critiqued ourselves. We needed someone to blame. Someone upon whom to lay the responsibility of our Coming. Maybe we were the problem, we considered. Perhaps our feet weren't fast enough. Unlike crewmen's feet, perhaps ours were too flat, too thick, too big to have carried us swiftly. Or maybe our lips had failed to deliver the message of impending bondage because, unlike theirs, ours were bold and bulging. We even considered that their abuse of our women might've been because our buttocks protruded. This would be true for some of our men, too. None of this had been a liability before. Our bodies had been our glory. We'd painted and adorned ourselves because we thought we were beautiful. Our decorated lips, hair, eyes, buttocks, feet, wide noses had all been expressions of self-adoration. Our body parts were the trademark, we believed, of a sacred, majestic people. Now the ugliness of our situation made us begin to loathe the body we'd once loved. It was a gradual occurrence at first, more a thought than a truth, but we knew that once planted, a seed soon reveals all that it bears.

The evening and the morning were the fifty-seventh day.

· · ·

On the fifty-eighth day, in the midst of a storm so angry we imagined sea gods locked in battle, a young pale lad of perhaps twelve rains came into our quarters and stood among us. He looked terrified but said nothing. With mouth covered and eyes wide, he stared at what must've been a horrific sight. We'd noticed him, sweeping and mopping the upper deck, but he'd been spared the experience of our holding station. Now, with neither permission nor preparation, he'd found his way to us. He might've been searching for a storage room or a food cellar or perhaps a compartment of weapons. Obviously he'd lost his way. Tears fell on his trembling left hand as he studied the room, lit only by the flickering candle in his right. Slowly, involuntarily, he moved among us, compelled by something far greater than mere curiosity. He reached forth a shivering, wet hand and touched black flesh, not with contempt and disdain, but with compassion and sympathy. He'd had no idea what his fathers had done. Now his fragile spirit couldn't bear the truth. For a moment, we felt for him as if he were our own. He had not chosen this legacy of hatred and abuse. Yet he would have it, and one day he'd probably be its perpetrator. He left suddenly and returned with a water bucket and quenched our thirst. We nodded our gratitude; he nodded his apology. Still, he did not leave. Our eyes begged him to free us but, of course, he could not. Yet his desire to do so stood in his tears. We nodded more vigorously until slowly, just as he'd come, he ascended the staircase and disappeared.

We thought of ourselves at his age, what we knew, what we wanted to know. Most of us, at twelve, were midway through our second manhood rite. We whispered about pretty girls and mocked ugly ones. We vied for elders' praise and admiration. We dreamed of homes full of children and livestock too plentiful to count. We raced to determine the fastest among us, then raced again to unseat him. We heard elders speak, although we didn't always care to listen. We were boys. Like any other boys. We wanted to know the world. So our people initiated us into knowledge of the universe. They taught us to read the movement of the stars in the sky. They showed us how, by the scent of the wind, to discern north from south. They taught us to bury our feet in the soil to learn the temperature of the earth. They insisted we study the behavior of ants to know the magic of community. They told us the wonder and spiritual qualities of fire, water, earth, and air. They taught us the differences and compliments between men and women. And with all this, they still said they knew nothing.

Some elders taught deeper levels of knowledge. Like how to interpret the song of the wind. And how to speak to diseases, of the body and the mind, and have them obey. One day, we would share this knowledge, they said, with our sons and daughters, and they with theirs. We were being initiated. Every boy in our village longed for his day in the forest, having dreamed of catching a wild beast without harming it. This was an assignment none escaped. Its purpose was never perfectly clear—since the beast was always set free—but the village applause bestowed immeasurable honor upon any boy who succeeded. Then, after our nineteenth or twentieth year, we'd be ushered into our last rite. This was when we'd learn the final secrets of manhood. We could not marry, have children, own a home, or acquire cattle until successful completion of this stage.

Most of us had never completed it. We wondered if we would be men in a new land. We wondered if pale people had standards of manhood different from our own. We wondered if even our own still applied since we'd been stolen and taken away. We wondered if perhaps the gods would exempt us from certain manifestations of character since we never learned them. We wondered so many things. Things about God we'd never been told. Things about nature we beheld but did not understand. Things about women we'd never experienced. Things about life we'd pondered but not comprehended. Now, on the ship, those things seemed unimportant, although weeks earlier they'd been our absolute preoccupation. We wondered whether the pale boy had completed his first initiation. Or whether his people even had such a system. If not, we thought, no wonder pale boys become murderous, treacherous men.

The evening and the morning were the fifty-ninth day.

. . .

On the sixtieth day, we awakened to the cries of a woman in labor. We knew the wailing. We'd heard it a thousand times. But not like this. Her howling contained no joy. Usually, in our village, when a mother bore a child, excitement reverberated in her screeching. Children gathered outside her hut, shouting with glee, beckoning forth the newborn babe. Once arrived, the infant was passed to the children first that they might welcome another playmate into the fold. Their noisy delight was the mother's comfort. Now, in bondage, our sister-mother would have to bear her child alone. We were surprised it had survived at all. As her belly ballooned, we knew she would bear not just any child, but a rare spirit. She had marched with us, suffered in the holdings on the coast with us, and now endured the nightmare of the ship. Most babies would've returned to the invisible place from which they come, but this one chose to join us nonetheless. This child was different. This child knew something. It was coming to say what we could not hear, to remind us of what we'd forgotten, to foretell a future we could not see.

The pain of what happened next lives in our collective memory. It mauls our souls each day. Yet it must be told. Silence guarantees no healing. It promises that the child's life would be forgotten and that its mission might, one day, be thought insignificant. Silence is the enemy of history, and history is all we have.

The child arrived hours later, replacing its mother's deep, dark wailing with jubilant cries. Even in our despair, we rejoiced. Some said boy, others said girl; we all said *ours*. When we came up for dancing the next day, we gawked at the most beautiful spirit the ancestors had ever sent. The child's skin glistened like coffee beans under a brilliant sun. And those eyes! They were the eyes of someone who had already seen what we were seeing, who could look inside us and know our hearts. Though only a day old, the child blinked and beheld each of us as if greeting old friends. We never knew the sex. We never asked. At the end of the dance, crewmen wrestled the child from its mother's flailing arms, and held it in the air. It cried a strange, moaning lament that lingered in our heads. It was something otherworldly, something reminiscent of the gods. There was no fear in its weeping. Only urgency. For us to listen. To hear beyond our circumstances. To know that one man cannot shape another man's destiny. We held our breath. The child's crying ceased. A crewman said something we could not understand, something surely to degrade us, then motioned to return the child to its mother. But instead of releasing the baby, he suddenly turned and buried a dagger in its belly. The mother fought like a trapped rhinoceros. Five shipmates wrestled to constrain her, and even then each panted with exhaustion. Some of us collapsed with agony. Others closed their eyes and begged ancestors to take him back quickly. Some looked across the sea and trembled. Others squeezed their bellies and cried. Some lunged toward the pale monster, but chains hindered them. Others called the names of our gods, furious that they would not come. And some stared at the bloody knife as if it might assume life and plunge itself into the murderer's flesh.

Belowdecks that day, we hummed a melody so dark it sent us into a trance. We hummed all night long. We hummed until we knew our little son or daughter was home. We hummed until our voices were raw and tender from constant vibration. We hummed for our sister-mother who would never be sane again. And we hummed that same melody for the rest of the journey whenever anguish stole our words. We gave thanks for one who came, merely for a moment, to remind us who we were. Who we *are*. We called the child Azubuike, which means "The past is your strength." We would see this child again, we believed.

By morning, the mother was gone, too. Safiya, one of the women from our village, told the story. She said a captor tossed the child into the ship's furnace. All the while, the mother's eyes rolled to the back of her head. Like a baby herself, groaning and moaning with pain, she lay limp against Safiya's breast. By her facial marks we knew she was Mandinka. Together, they sat on deck, beneath a starlit sky, holding each other as only women can, when suddenly the mother raised her head, looked into Safiya's eyes, and nodded knowingly. She dragged herself to the ship's edge and plunged into the water. This was the second child she had borne but could not have. Now she would find her children, somewhere in the realm of the spirits, and love them the way a mother should. We wept as we heard the story.

The evening and the morning were the sixty-second day.

. . .

One might think this episode ruined our resolve. It did not. It became fuel for our survival. We knew a day of reckoning would come. It was the promise of the universe.

More of us died. Diseases, melancholy, and big fish all took their portion. But more of us lived, too. Each day after the sixty-third, we began to speak our names aloud. It became a collective ritual, a daily roll call, an announcement of the yet living. Someone would beat his planks like a drum and say his own name three times. That was the sign. Then the rest of us would join in, beating our planks with our fists and speaking our names in succession: Amadi, Kayode, Yafeu, Kwesi, Abubakar, Dumi, Enyinnaya, Atiba, Ogbonna, Bekitembe, , Shamba, Oluremi, Ayzize, Chitope, Najja, Damani, Oifie, Ato, Giunëur, Ousman, Yoro, Chukwudi, Akintunde, Akinyele, Akinfola, Ajani, Bem, Boseda, Wole, Oshundwaqueke, Alatanga, Tafataona, Tamba , Tefase, Mensah, Ansa, Olufemi, Bataraishe, Adika, Muomaife, Ogunwale, and more. When there was silence, we knew a warrior had fallen. We didn't always remember his name, but we ceased drumming long enough to honor his memory. Then, fists pounded again until every living soul made his presence known. Above deck, our women did the same once our calling subsided. They shouted their names that we might hear: Citalala, Ama, Tegbe, Naki, Mabasi, Pepukaiye, Ifetayo, Chisanganda, Omolara, Akili, Camara, Jaha, Anela, Kariamu, Zinzele, Oluyassa, Osizwe, Makata, Efuru, Binta, Nilaja, Olutobi, Titilayo, Enomwoyi, Anoa, Iyabode, Aminata, Ayodele, Yewande, Nsombi, Buseje, Dofi, Nakpangi, Folasade, Ijeoma, Dzigbodi, Nazapa, Adenike, Monji, Kwansimah, Lebene, Ngozi, Wahde, and more. We struck planks once between each name. There were other names, too. Far too many to recall now. Yet with each name we nodded and knew someone had survived.

When rations ran low, we suspended roll call and conserved our energy. Sometimes, we barely ate once a day. Even then, we were given a mere handful of paste. As our stomachs growled, we spent countless, numbing hours trying to imagine where we were going and what it looked like. Were there trees? Grasslands? Wild beasts like our own? Were there rivers and streams? Forests? Fruits? There had to be pale women, of course. And what of their girls? Surely they were kinder than crewmen had been. We wondered, too, why these people even wanted us. What justified killing half of us for the other half? Whatever the business, couldn't they do it themselves? We had no answers. Only questions framed in fury. How long would our gods let this madness continue? How would we ever commemorate those lost at sea? Was mush the only food pale people ate? Did captors assault their women the way they assaulted ours? Did they plunge their way through other pale men without permission? *Allah? Oludumare? Chukwu? Who are these people?*

And who were we? We sighed. With each passing day, our memories merged into one gigantic past about which we could only dream. Even our surnames disintegrated as we tried, with all our might, simply to learn the first names of the one lying next to us. He was a brother now. He would be the uncle to our sons and daughters. The brother-in-law to our wives. The grandfather who would tell the story to the next generation. By the sixty-fifth day, we were a new people. Our elders would've been proud. First, that we had not all died. Then, that we had chosen to fight together. That we had used our names to speak life into each others' despondent hearts. That we had put aside tribal tensions and stood as one people. That even when others jumped overboard, we called their names and sealed their memories in our minds. Yes, they would've nodded their approval. That, once again, our dances sustained us in battle. That our tongues and throats joined forces and created life-affirming melodies. That we'd tried, with all our might, to get free. And they would've even been proud that the pale boy gave us drink to quench our thirst. They would've given him a name, surely, to celebrate his role in our survival. And perhaps the elders would've been proudest of all that we'd never forgotten them.

On the sixty-sixth day, crewmen danced up on deck, drinking strong drink and playing loud music with their instruments. Maybe they rejoiced, we assumed, because they thought the rebels among us had been destroyed. We didn't know. But we heard ranting and raving, shouting and stomping, as if all their worries had vanished. The celebration lasted far into the night. We knew because, unlike other days, they did not close and lock the latch to our compartment. Moonlight cast shadows of drunken crewmen, stumbling back and forth, grabbing our women but releasing them playfully. We even saw the silhouette of our pale angel, standing at the top of the stairs, glaring belowdecks but afraid to defy his fathers. Amidst the noise, we searched each other's curious faces. We feared their joy would be our sorrow.

It was. We were left chained for five days. No dancing, no sexual abuse, no verbal degradation. Something was definitely amiss. We sensed it in our spirits. But there was nothing we could do. Too nervous to hum, we lay awake, day and night, in stark silence and nauseating defecation, hoping desperately for a sign of what was to come.

On the seventy-first day, the sign came. We were rustled, like corralled cattle, above deck. Certainly we'd come to dance, we thought. Mostly we were grateful simply to stand, as our joints needed exercise. But when we lifted our heads and glanced about, we gasped and stumbled in horror. Our chains rattled. Our hearts beat faster. There, in the distance, was the pale man's land.

This was The Coming.

PART II

The landscape looked strange and overcrowded, with curious plants and bushes so green they seemed unreal. A bright, beaming sun hovered above, like a proud parent over an obedient child, radiating light in every direction. The flowers were deep red, orange, yellow, purple, and white. This vegetation stood amidst peculiar, awkward-looking trees. We frowned at them. They were tall and lean, like young unmarried men, and bare—only at the top did spindly extensions sprout forth, with the miniature arms of an acacia bush. There were other trees, too, more like our own, but smaller and less demanding. Behind them were rolling hills covered with dense, tall grass. Our cattle would've been pleased. The air was heavy with moisture, as if it were about to rain, but there were no clouds. All we could think about was what this place would mean for us, and what new forms our bondage might take.

Soon, captors splashed us with seawater, and we cried from the sting of salt in our open wounds. They were preparing us for something we couldn't have imagined.

Other boats advanced from various directions. An

ominous feeling overwhelmed us. Pale people stood along the coast, waving at kinsmen long the seaside. We beheld their women, covered in cloth from the neck down. They smiled, although they appeared uncomfortable, wrapped so tightly at the waist we wondered how they breathed. There were men, too, dressed more neatly than our crewmen. Some sported pants that stopped at the knee and shirts with extra cloth around the neck and wrists. We surely would've laughed had we been home. But we were not home. So we stared, overcome with dread and the frightening anticipation of what was to come.

Sailors erupted with joy. We didn't understand their tongue, but we knew they spoke of extraordinary profits and pretty women with whom they would share it. They danced around us like we were mere objects of cargo.

Small boats, more square than oval, raced to meet the captors' ship. There had to be five or six of them, dashing across the water like anxious fish prepared to devour a meal. Crewmen, more drunk than sober, stumbled among us, pointing to those they seemingly preferred. A light wind blew as we huddled together in horror. The monsters of the sea that swam alongside us the day before were gone now. We were utterly alone. And terrified. Captors mocked our vulnerable lot by feigning fear and shivering, then laughing at us. There was nowhere to

run, nowhere to swim, no land with which we were familiar. They had brought us to a new world, and we had no
choice but to be there. Stripped of home and dreams, we
were about to be introduced to a life far worse than what
we'd already known.

With an air of excitement, well-dressed pale men
climbed into the vessel and, in broad daylight, examined
our bodies. They poked and prodded our flesh. They
touched our genitals. They bent us over and checked our
anuses for the bloody flux. They pried open our mouths
to check our teeth. They paid sailors money for our bodies. They bought Chisanganda and left Abuto behind. He
wailed as he watched his dream unfold. His arms and legs
jerked with the strength of the mighty giraffe, but the
chains were stronger. Chisanganda heaved in her weeping as two new captors dragged her away. Abuto collapsed to the floor of the ship. Nothing we said or did
soothed him. Before disappearing, Chisanganda raised
her hand and waved quickly. Yet, blinded with grief, Abuto did not see her.

We were examined head to toe, all of us, the way
hunters examine a freshly killed carcass. We were
touched with uncaring hands, frowned upon because of
our stench, and sneered at because we were obviously
different. They parted our thick, coarse hair with their
small, pink fingers in desperate search of some miniature

deficiency. They inspected our eyes without looking at us. They seemed to be probing for irregularities or abnormalities of which we were unaware. While their shame was hidden with layers of clothing, ours was exposed without reservation. They explored us as if they actually owned us! They caressed our women's breasts and nodded with sensual approval. They bore our penises in the palms of their hands and grunted with pleasure. Our trembling went unnoticed. Our quivering meant nothing to them. Buyers gawked and grabbed their preferences and wouldn't let go. The undesirable were ignored. We learned quickly what they didn't like: full, pronounced lips, wide flat noses, the darkest complexions. And what they did: full, pronounced buttocks; narrow, oval faces; lean, chiseled torsos; hips that promised spreading; small, perky breasts. A man's large feet, thick thighs, and massive hands. They exchanged money for our flesh. And smiled.

This was The Coming.

. . .

Those they bought they took right away. Within seconds they were loosed of their chains and ushered off the boat. That was the last time we saw them. Each of them turned and looked back with sorrow. We were being separated once again from those we'd grown to love. Most of us had survived only because we'd chosen to fight for one another, because we'd decided, together, not to die. Now we were divided again, into fractions of the original fraction. We were diminished into a mere band of bound men and women when, in truth, we'd come from great nations of thousands. Life had changed in one season on the ship, and we weren't sure now what tomorrow would bring.

From the corners of our eyes, we saw the pale boy hiding behind a barrel of grain. His bottom lip shuddered each time one of us was sold away. His eyes begged us to believe he was not one of them. To know that, if he'd had his way, he would've set us free. To trust that if he could've forced his fathers to take us home he would've. We believed him. But his mouth said nothing, and we understood why. Any gesture of kindness shown us during the journey had been met with severe punishment. So the boy was right to believe he could do nothing. Still, his eyes exposed that he wanted to.

Even in our misery, we saw the beauty of his heart. It bore the strength of elephant's tusks and the majesty of peacock's wings. It had quenched our thirsts that fateful day and assured us that spirit can dwell in pale flesh, too. We didn't know what would become of him, but we knew his potential to change the world—if it didn't change him first. He'd have to defy everything he knew, to go against every example his fathers had set, in order to realign what they had misaligned, but we held out hope that he would. For us. For himself. For the balance of the earth. We had survived, so anything was possible.

After that day we never saw him again. But we remembered him. We hoped he would someday heal diseases lurking in the hearts of his people. He was a flicker of light in a dark world, and we knew why he'd been sent. And by whom. We prayed he'd discover it, too, and eventually mend his people's brokenness. Like all the others who'd died along the way, he lived in our collective memory of those who'd sacrificed for our survival. A few blinked at him, hiding behind the barrel, trusting in their hearts as they were dragged away that he wouldn't become one of them.

As for the rest of us, mere skin and bones, we were returned to our holding places belowdecks. With so many gone, the room felt vacant and hollow, like a cave. We were scattered throughout the hull without the luxury of human contact. We, the undesirable, were left to ponder what further abuses we could endure. Knowing nothing else to do, we brooded in silence. And waited.

Hours later, crewmen entered with platters of fresh food. They loosed our shackles and pointed to the victuals and nodded. Then, with the exception of two, they left. We feared what seemed too good to be true, so at first we didn't touch anything. However, starvation propelled us on, and, slowly, we began to consume foods we'd never known. Some of the meat tasted slightly familiar, but the fruits and vegetables were entirely new. They were tasty, so we ate our fill. It had been months since we'd had a decent meal; thus, we consumed everything with a vengeance. We considered that it might be poisoned, that this might be yet another means of our destruction, but hunger would not be denied. If we died, we thought, at least we'd die full. Two crewmen, with pointed rifles, stood guard over us but never interrupted our feasting. When we finished, they called for others, and together they reattached our chains and returned us to our horizontal cages. It was all very strange.

We remained in the dungeon of that ship for weeks, still counting days. The vessel swayed slightly with the movement of the water, but did not sail. Each morning and evening, we were given food in great abundance. Fruits of every kind and sweetness, vegetables of every possible color, meats favorable to our tongue. We still didn't know why. It mattered less each day. We regained our strength. Some even began to look like themselves again. We believed our gods had moved upon the hearts of our captors. We had more water than we could drink. Several times a day, a tin cup met our mouths and we swallowed until satisfied. Some of the foods, we later learned, were mangoes, breadfruit, coconut, guava, jack-fruit, papaya, pineapple, cassava, callaloo, ackee, arrow-root, figs, cabbage, plantain, rice, squash, sweet potato, and yam. We had rice and yam, too, but not like this yam. Each meal also consisted of healthy portions of chicken or pork and other unidentifiable meats. Our bellies were full, but our hearts were empty and laced with gloom. We didn't know what to think. Or what our futures held. Or what became of those left behind. Or what they would do with those they took away. Or how, now, to plan our escape with so many gone. Or whether we should try to escape at all, knowing nothing about their land. We began to believe that they had fed us simply to distract us. To create in our spirits complacency that might usurp our desire to fight. If so, their plan did not work. In the midnight hour, we whispered across blank spaces, trying desperately to plan our getaway. We promised our gods that, if we were successful, we'd tell the story of our unthinkable journey and remind our people never to lose faith. We made all sorts of promises on that ship.

The plan failed before execution. We couldn't agree on what to do, and, as strangers to the land, we didn't know where to go or in which direction to run. Or even how to navigate the ship. We weren't strangers to the Great Waters, but we knew nothing about the steering of their boats. So we thought it best to wait until the ancestors or God bent advantages in our favor.

One day, rain fell continuously, hour after creeping hour, until we were sure the whole world had flooded. Droplets danced on the upper deck, creating a rhythm so strong, so intoxicating, so melodious we had no choice but to close our eyes and listen. The constant tapping sounded like a thousand djembe's being beaten simultaneously, causing the very ship to tremble. Water fell so hard the vessel vibrated. We were not afraid. Thunder and lightning accompanied the rain and quieted our anxious hearts. Then we understood. We knew the message. A woman from our village voiced it. Amidst the noise, she bellowed, "We shall not all die. We shall live again. In a new land." She paused, then continued: "And we shall prosper and teach the souls of men the ways of God." Water from the sky, she explained, was an ancestral libation to those we'd lost along the way. They had not been forgotten. Each drop was a soul, a mother or father gone before their work was done. Oh, how it rained! Together, the chaotic sounds of the heavens droned a healing melody we hadn't heard since we'd left home. It was beautiful. Our spirits opened up. For a moment, we stepped beyond our chains and saw ourselves again. We were strong. We were mighty. We were gods. We belonged to ourselves. We belonged to each other. We belonged to the land. Our spirits were free. They had bought our flesh, but not our souls.

It rained all night long. Some hummed, just loud enough to create melody in the room. We were the last, but we were here. We had endured.

This was The Coming.

The evening and the morning were the ninety-second day.

. . .

By morning, when the rain ceased, our frustration and fury multiplied. Where were we? What had they done with our comrades? What were they planning to do with us?

By now, many of us knew each other's names. We'd called them daily, as a ritual reminder of our existence. We'd learned to shout "Yeabo" or "Ashe," which means "It is so," as the verbal affirmation of each life. The collective chorus elicited the only joy of our days. It was beautiful, hearing the refrain repeated by the Ashanti and the Akan, the Mende and the Fulani. These voices had generally never joined together in ritual space, but now they rang out in unity, summoning life-sustaining, communal power. It was a chorus of determination, a merging of differences we never thought we'd see. Yet we needed it. We knew much sorrow. Out of more than 300 captives, there were hardly 100 left. Our confidants, our midnight companions, had been sold away. Most of us lay abandoned, with no one on either side. Only silence between. In some ways, it was worse than the noise of the sea. It made us hear rats scurrying beneath us and captors murmuring above. It made us know loneliness without the comfort of a friend. It taught us to go within for answers though we'd been trained to seek others. It made long hours longer. It intensified the buzzing of flies and gnats around our heads. We screamed as the irritation drove us mad. Some shook their heads so hard their brains loosened. They cried and fought, but they didn't win. Eventually, they surrendered to the annoyance and let the insects have their way. Our death toll leveled. We ate and dreamed of home.

Eventually, we spoke our longings: "Our children shall laugh and play beneath the baobab tree again!" "Our healers will cleanse us of all we've suffered." "Wait till our warriors come together and rescue us!" "The griots have their work cut out for generations!" "We must learn why our gods let this happen and correct ourselves before our altars!" "We must be careful not to become like these people!" "When we get home, we must begin the children's initiation sooner!" "I need some pepper soup!" And on and on until, in our imaginations, we had reconstructed our world. We saw hunters sitting in total harmony, sharpening arrows and tightening bows. We saw weavers weaving baskets so meticulous they carried water. We saw dancers creating movements that mimicked the stride of the flamingo and the gallop of the zebra. We saw men, strong as rhinos, carrying logs for building. We saw, in every direction, children dashing behind compounds, playing games their great grandparents had played. We saw farmers with backs bent, toiling over vegetables that would sustain us all. We saw old men, sitting in the shade, smoking pipes and telling stories of bygone days of glory. We saw old women, whispering and laughing about the truth of those stories. We felt the evening breeze bring relief from the relentless heat of the day. We saw the Great Council pondering issues until everyone nodded agreeably. We heard hyenas laughing in the distance. We heard lions roaring. We heard babies enter the world. We heard weeping when elders left. We heard young men fighting and arguing playfully over frivolous things. We heard young women chuckling about their uncertain futures. We saw the life we'd once taken for granted.

This vision propelled us on. It made us believe that, although constricted and isolated, we were not destroyed. Hours later, when crewmen entered with another feast of fattening, we swallowed meats, vegetables, and fruits until our bellies protruded. We knew captors' motives were not pure. We'd been together long enough to know they desired only our destruction.

Waiting and wondering took its toll. In the darkness, some of us screamed and yanked our chains, just as before, until shreds of flesh dangled from ankles and wrists. Blood stained iron shackles. Even then, the screaming continued. We didn't know what they were thinking, those brothers whose minds left their heads. We reached toward them, but couldn't touch. We called their names, over and over—Yoro! Ato! Chukwudi—but their spirits were too far gone to connect. One man, Alatanga, screamed until blood spewed from his throat. There were no words in his lament; only the wailing of a soul at its edge. He beat his head against the plank. Blood dripped from the corner of his mouth and collected on the floor, carrying his life force to an everlasting place. We were now even fewer than the day before.

The evening and the morning were the ninety-third day.

. . .

We regained our weight and our countenance. We noticed new faces among crewmen. Many of them, too, had died along the way. When they tossed our bodies into the sea, they often flung one of their own. Some died from diseases that had consumed us. Some were killed when we fought to free ourselves. Some were cut down for insubordination. Some were forced to starve that we, the cargo, might live. Some, we later learned, jumped overboard, too—once they discovered the fullness of what they'd signed up for. Their hearts couldn't take it. Some died in drunken brawls that got out of hand. And some died simply from dehydration. Truth was, they died as we died. It made sense. The universe demands life for life.

On the ninety-fourth day, still in harbor, we were taken above deck to dance. We'd been danced at sea, but not like this. With whips and cat-o-nine-tails in hand, new crewmen struck us until we jumped and moved to avoid their blows. Having eaten so heavily without moving for days, we passed gas as our joints creaked with pain. Many clutched their sides from intense cramps. Crewmen mimicked and mocked our steps. Positioned among us, they flung their arms and jumped about like crazy men. Sweat poured from their brows, as from ours, and still they compelled us on. A few of us fainted from the intensity. We must've danced for hours. At the start, the sun shone directly above; when we stopped, it was far to the right. We didn't have the strength to return belowdecks. Instead, we collapsed right there, exhausted, as we panted for precious breath. Some vomited black bile so disgusting it made others sick. A few wept because they couldn't catch their breaths. Two or three prayed that Death would stop teasing and simply complete its work. Several massaged sore ankles, streaked with blood. We wanted to rise up, but didn't have the strength. We should've asked for God's help, but so many had stopped believing. We now questioned everything we'd been taught about spirits, the heavens, God, righteousness. When it really mattered, nothing we believed had saved us.

At the break of day, the ship jolted. We awoke, startled. Where were we going? Was it possible they were taking the rest of us home? The day before, while torturing us in the dance, they had washed out our hold for only the second time since we'd been captured. They returned to deck with their noses and mouths covered. Some were nauseous, vomiting and stumbling as they ascended the wooden staircase. The hold wasn't clean, we'd soon discover, but it smelled of vinegar instead of feces for a change, and that alone was a relief—for the day or two it lasted.

The ship felt less steady than before. Perhaps vacant space allotted room for our bodies to roll and tumble as the ship rocked along. So many brothers and sisters were gone. Only the chains held us in place. Without them, we would've been a pile of black bodies, strewn across the hull, covered in our own waste. With them, we were bound to a place and time, which we did not understand. Yet without resources and advocates to fight for us, we did what we had done for the past several months—we grunted, cried, hummed, and waited.

Several of our young women and men began to exhibit strange symptoms. Greenish-yellow, milky discharge coming from their vaginas and penises. Sores on their lips, in their mouths, in their rectums. Any movement of waste caused excruciating pain. They burned inside and cried out for relief. Fevers and sharp pains in their lower bellies made their living a nightmare. One young man's lips were so lesioned he could not eat. Pus and blood seeped into his throat, reminding him constantly that he'd been some captor's favorite. Shame drove him into the sea. Others suffered more each day with something new: rashes on their hands, throbbing headaches, strange lumps on their necks. We believed their infection came from captors' lust. There was nothing our precious comrades could do. For some, the sores and pain went away. At least at first. Then, as if to mock them, other parts of their bodies malfunctioned until, in an attempt to protect their cargo, crewmen either cast them into the sea or burned them alive.

For those who survived, disgrace lounged upon their faces. It left them wounded in the soul. These were women and men—proud, strong, young, agile—having served as the repository of our enemy's vile desire. Humiliation darkened their countenance, causing them to look away when we tried to love them. Sores and accompanying illnesses only reminded them that they had been defeated. Many hung their heads so low we hardly saw their eyes. There was little hope of recovery. They could never find their beauty again. Some awaited the opportunity to leave this realm, and when it came, they took it without hesitation. The few who remained, those who had been violated but not consumed with sexual diseases, sought the path back to themselves, struggling through mountains of self-hatred and silence, unable to hear anything about the power of the spirit over the flesh. When, days later, they lifted their heads, shame still lumbered in their eyes. It never went away. It was all so devastating.

A crewman in white clothes visited our compartment every couple of days. He examined our bodies, staring into our eyes not as a fellow human being but as one commissioned to study them. He touched us in ways similar to our medicine men back home, but he seemed to possess no healing power. He offered no herbs or drinks to correct our ailing bodies, and he never laid hands on us to extract illnesses or calm our troubled emotions. He hardly stayed among us more than a moment or two. His nose was covered with a white cloth, so he worked with only one hand. He was the one who plugged anuses of those infected with the bloody flux. If he was a healer, we thought, he was young in the craft and definitely needed more time with a master.

Accompanying him was the man they called Frank. We grew to despise him. He'd been with us from the beginning of our journey, and he guarded us until the end. Sometimes, with a cat-o-nine-tails, he beat us for no good reason. Even while we lay belowdecks, chained and consumed with misery, he often came and displayed his power by screaming at us and lashing our flesh. Most painful was that he was one of us. He bore the marks of the Asanti. We tried to reason with him, to make him see himself, but the sound of our voices only increased his fury. It was as if captors had extracted his brain and replaced it with one of their own. In their presence, he was softer, kinder, more conscious of his being; in ours, he was nasty, violent, and wicked. We asked for his name, but for an answer he spat upon us.

His pride increased whenever he demeaned us, especially in the presence of crewmen. He'd strike our flesh then, after each blow, glance at their faces. Their affirmation excited him. If they nodded, he nodded. If they smiled, he smiled. There was nothing he wouldn't do to win their applause. He seemed to believe he wasn't one of us. We were fascinated by his blindness. How did he fail to see that they'd kill him, too, if his allegiance ever waned?

After leaving port for the second time, we began to disregard him. This increased his wrath. In his native tongue, he said, "You are nothing but animal guts! If you don't obey me, you're going to die! You're here because you're weak and stupid!" His blows left streaks of open flesh across our bodies. Worst of all, when his temper flared beyond control, he muted voices so completely some never spoke again. Those who pleaded with him to return to his original self had their throats sliced with a blade that left them speechless for the rest of their lives. As far as we know he never repented. He spoke the captor's tongue. He spoke our tongues. He walked with confidence and assurance, as if he owned the ship. His steps were heavy and loud, like those of a fat man, although he was average size. His demeanor smelled of arrogance; his character stank like rotten meat. We would've killed him as quickly as we had killed the ship's crewmen. But then we would've been guilty, once again, of shedding our own people's blood. We sighed heavily. There was no way to win.

The evening and the morning were the ninety-eighth day.

• • •

Our only clarity was that he was Asanti—those warring souls rumored to love battle more than peace. Their king was reported to have the heads of enemies staked on posts outside his palace. Only maggots and birds were allowed to touch them. The Asanti weren't all rogues, however. Among them, one could find the most skilled archers in the world. Tales swirled concerning those who could strike a bird through the heart mid-flight. Everyone knew of their reputation for fishing with bows and arrows. When others caught nothing, they went home with heavy strings of fish. It was said that they feasted practically every week. Their only weakness, or perhaps the one we feared most, was that they loved war. Any spirit that loves war loves death. The Asanti man had parallel vertical marks beneath his eyes, so some thought he could've been Fante or Ewe since they, too, mark likewise. But most agreed he was Asanti. We dared not ask. Rather, we held our peace while he became our enemy.

There had been others, too. At the onset of our journey, while being transferred onto the ship, we recalled seeing Africans along the coast, bartering native goods such as beeswax and gold, kola nuts and ivory, for pale trader's guns and spices. Our shoreline was a veritable open-air market. Captors, like some of our men, were most interested in their own economic gain. *Greed cares not who carries it,* our *jali* used to say. *It simply longs to live. And it can live in the heart of any man.* We knew this. In every village, including our own, there were those who'd acquired things simply to have them. Elders said that their spirits were fragile, that someone had failed to show them their worth, so they needed the applause of objects. We pitied them. But after a while, we praised them, too. The allure of things caught our eye and made many of us desire what none of us needed. We began to throw away food simply because we didn't want it. We crafted so much garb we couldn't wear it all. We made huts large enough for ten when there were only five. This was not everyone, but it was enough of us to plant the seeds of excess among a people who generally valued simplicity. We had invited this plague of materialism and it had come. Captors had come, too, undetected, unshrouded by our suspicion, precisely because they'd wanted what we'd wanted—life in abundance. Now we didn't want any of it. We simply wanted to go home.

The evening and the morning were the ninety-ninth day.

• • •

Two women, whose bodies serviced captors nightly, told of the captain writing in a large ledger. They weren't sure of its contents, but he wrote every night, they said, with great focus and fervor. Some of us were writers, too, but, as a people, we were masters of the spoken word. Our crowning feature was our storytelling. Jali could weave tales for hours without ever losing anyone's attention. We wondered whether, in his big book, the captain was creating tales for his people or simply recording daily events. Illuminated by candlelight, he wrote slowly, deliberately, they said, as if afraid of making an error. If he was interrupted, his anger flared and someone would be flogged. A few times, our women watched him write as his tears fell on the pages. They never knew why. The most plausible explanation came from one of our boys who said the captain's tears fell because, having treated us so, he would never see God. We wondered if, one day, one of us might write about what we'd seen and endured. We needed a record, we thought, of our experience, lest the day come when our children found our story implausible. We needed a book to tell the world of our glorious kingdoms and our spirit-filled rituals, less people believe we'd always been enslaved. But who would write it? And what tongue would they use? And where would they begin? No one would believe we'd spent weeks—no, months—on a ship, bound with chains, with barely enough food to fill our palms. Or that the Great Waters had been poisoned with our blood. Or that we'd learned songs without words that had kept our spirits centered. One of us would have to write a book so the world would know who we were.

The next day, several were found burning with black fever. The captain ordered them thrown overboard. We heard mournful cries as bodies splashed against the water's surface. Then, for the first time, we heard a crewman announce their departure: "Number 123, a man, gone." "Number 65, a man, gone." "Number 88, a woman, gone." "Number 13, a boy, gone." They'd surely said this before, when bodies were cast into the sea, but we didn't understand them then. Now we knew enough of their language to piece together the meaning of some of their words. We were merely cargo—counted items to be sold away. Perhaps this was the price we had to pay for having ignored our own wisdom.

Once again, there were days when the wind disappeared. The boat sat still as a gourd upon the earth. We knew we were not going home. We did not smell, in the distance, our rivers, our land, our people. We were somewhere far, far away. The air was thick and heavy. Our air had been thin and sweet, moving easily across open plains and carrying the aroma of fruits and flowers. We saw ourselves laughing and playing as mango juice dried on our hands and faces. Then we'd dash to the brook and play in the water until we were cool and clean. We could hear it, the brook, singing a melody that echoed throughout the forest. We loved the song of the brook. Some of our boys could mimic it so perfectly that their voices were integrated into rituals when we needed the brook's healing power. We heard, now, the song of the open seas, but it was not the same. It was harsh and rough, full of discordant harmonies and unpleasant dissonances. It had its beauty, yet we wanted our song back—the soft strain of the brook—flowing easily among us. We feared we'd never hear it again.

Just above our heads, captors laughed and lounged cheerfully. They didn't feel our grief. They didn't know our sorrow. Music and dancing accompanied their glee. We wondered how, in the midst of death and disease, they could be so joyful. Then, slowly, overtime, we heard words we assumed to be their names: Jack. Nickolas. Alex. Charles. John. Wesley. David. Michael. Henry. George. Thomas. We wondered what they meant. Didn't their names scold them for treating us like beasts? Didn't someone's name remind him to act like God? Didn't "John" or perhaps "David" mean *love the stranger?* Didn't their names mean *something?* Maybe that was the root of their behavior, we thought. Maybe they had been given names without meanings. They even called the Asanti

beast one of their names: Frank. He answered with en-
thusiasm. They couldn't have called him his original
name. His spirit wouldn't have supported his despicable
behavior. So, as Frank, he separated himself from his purpose and thus became a tool for our destruction. If only
we knew his real name, we could've called him back to his
center, back to his sacred self. But as long as that name remained a mystery, he could be like the pale man.

The evening and the morning were the One hundred
and third day.

• • •

The wind returned with a vengeance, rocking the ship
and causing waves to slap against it. Each movement re-
opened scabs across our backs and buttocks. With so
many gone, we had very little comfort. We felt more
alone than ever. Our hopes of a revolt faded. Empty
spaces meant we had no human buffers from the storm.
Our worn, tired bodies tossed like blades of grass in the
wind as the ship twisted and turned from the rocky seas.
Some vomited. Some cursed angrily. Some closed their
eyes and prayed the storm would pass. Some hummed to
still their turbulent bellies. Some envisioned how they'd
kill crewmen. Frank, too. Some imagined, amidst furious
waves, the faces of those who'd met Death in the waters.

Some spoke aloud to ancestors, begging for intervention. Some said nothing at all.

Rain drizzled through the upper deck, pouring upon us in miniature waterfalls. We opened our mouths and drank. The cold water quenched our thirst at first, then became an irritant. Half naked and shivering, we were drenched and miserable. And the rain kept coming. We'd rarely seen a storm so relentless. During our rainy season, water fell each day to nourish the earth and sustain our crops. Sometimes it rained hard. But never like this. "The gods are angry," some said. "Our lesson is not complete." They must've been right. It rained continuously for the next two days. One man shuddered and screamed until he went out of his mind. Others tried to hum, in order to warm their chilly bodies and keep their spirits calm, but we were too upset to sing collectively. The most we could do was breathe deeply and beg the storm to pass. Of course, we couldn't sleep. Every few hours, someone called out names, hoping not to lose family members we'd made. An Akan man shouted "Yeabo!" repeatedly, declaring his will to survive. We were downtrodden, but we had not surrendered the fight.

When the storm subsided and the ship settled, we fell into a deep sleep. Our spirits wandered other realms, discovering lifeforms we'd never known and dancing with loved ones we thought we'd never see again. They told us that death was only a fleeting moment, that there was no pain at all. They said that in the blinking of an eye, they'd arrived in another time and place. They told us not to fear. Whatever we endured couldn't last forever. They told us that when we died, we'd see God and understand everything.

We awakened to shouts and curses. It was time to eat. Many of our stomachs were too upset for food. Others didn't want it. They had decided not to swallow another morsel of the captor's mush. They were going to the land of endless day. Now we were three fewer than before. Their bodies went overboard.

Several recalled the story of the first time our people were captured and taken away. It was centuries before pale people arrived. The others were brown, some as dark as us, with shiny, straight, black hair. They, too, raided our villages and plundered our culture. They took our people northward, across the great Sahara, into a land always desperate for rain. The story seemed too fantastic to be true. According to legend, these invaders slaughtered our people simply for amusement. Before they were defeated, they had taken more than nine million souls. The story was too big for our imagination. We did not believe it. The storytellers said, "This is pure truth!" They begged us to hear and to understand why others wanted our strengths, our gifts. We dismissed them as overzealous lovers of ourselves, as artists committed to the art of speech. Then, on ships, we wept as storytellers' voices echoed in our consciousness. We were living again the tale we'd thought impossible.

The evening and the morning were the one hundred and sixth day.

· · ·

Talking practically ceased. Shouts of anger and protest dwindled to mere whispers. We felt overwhelmed and belittled. A few grunted and beat planks but, for the most part, we closed our mouths and shivered with shame. We couldn't believe we'd let ourselves be captured by those with half our might. We were warriors! We were people of extraordinary achievements. Men and women of triumphant courage. Now we realized that, amidst those great accomplishments, we had missed something critical, something that would've saved us.

A Wolof man told us what it was. Earlier in the journey, we had wasted considerable time arguing. Whether from stepping on another's fingers on the way to dancing or disagreeing about the course we should take to overthrow the ship or fussing about whether it would be correct to spill Frank's blood or haggling over whether to set the ship ablaze and destroy ourselves in the process, tempers flared and our character diminished. We knew better. We'd been taught that character is never situational. So, again, we'd failed our own teaching. We unleashed anger upon one another because there was no one else to bear it. And each time we fell below our standard, the Wolof man lifted his hands, spread his fingers apart, and shook his head sadly. He never said a word. Most didn't notice. Not until mid-journey, when, after a fierce encounter between two men of once-warring tribes, he screamed so loudly it frightened us. Still he didn't speak. He lifted his hands and spread his fingers wide. Angry, bulbous eyes forced our attention. Then, slowly, he brought the fingers together until they melded into a tight fist. We understood. They had captured us because we had been divided. That was our lesson.

From that day forward, all bickering calmed. We had fought each other, back home *and* on the ship, for reasons we thought legitimate, but now they seemed silly and unimportant. Like going to war over territorial rights and hunting lands. Or the bride price of women thought priceless. Or the killing of someone for stealing part of our harvest when we had more than we could eat! Or taking another life over disputes concerning fishing rights and river boundaries. We had even killed because of perceived disrespect. It seemed so foolish now. We had been concerned with complex, invisible knowledge, when we should've also been searching for God in simple things. Senior elders said this. We'd wanted to impress our neighbors, to feel superior to them, when living in harmony with them was the greater achievement. We shook our heads, the few who remained. This was what the Wolof man meant. Our strength was our unity. Our lives depended upon it. We understood. Every day he repeated the gesture until the image of his raised fist lingered in our minds.

Yeabo!

The evening and the morning were the one hundred and seventh day.

· · ·

As the ship sailed on, we made music once again with the means of our bondage. Our bodies swayed with the violent seas; chains and irons began to sing. The melody had been imperceptible at first, but then, as more of us died, empty chains rattled louder, accompanying our mournful cries. A dark, hollow tune echoed throughout the ship. The singing chains were complimented by the thunderous slamming of neck rings against wooden planks. It was torturous, but the sounds comforted a desperate, isolated people. Soon, we created an ensemble of drums and shakers. Someone banged handcuffs together, and others quickly joined in. Every manacle in the room vibrated as an instrument of our survival. Our propensity for melody had accompanied us through the entire journey. Even in bondage, we were still who we were. They could bind us, but they could not extract rhythm from our souls.

We would not all die. If we could make our shackles sing, we could heal our spirits. We could create a new self in a new land. We declared it so in our minds. We said it in our hearts every time we played those chains. And we made them sing each night until we reached our destination.

The next time they brought us above deck to dance, we saw land in the distance. It was too far away to see particulars, but we had a feeling it was the last stop. There were less than ninety of us left. We were weary and despondent. The dance that day was a movement of zombies overwhelmed. We looked drunk, surely, stumbling into one another and swinging arms to a rhythm our feet didn't recognize. Within half an hour, we were returned to the belly of the ship.

Our nerves unraveled. How would we make a life in a place we'd never seen, never been, never heard of? How would we honor those lost along the way? How would we maintain dignity and character among people who despised us? Wouldn't they continue, even on land, their campaign to destroy our souls?

We were no longer simply the Fon, the Ibo, the Hausa, the Yoruba, the Ewe. We were something other than the Ashanti, the Fante, The Fulani, the Serere, and the Mende. Something new, some combination of them all, some blending of culture and spirit our elders wouldn't have recognized. We were a different people now, with roots in every place we had trod. We were *one* tree, with branches reaching in every possible direction and leaves sprouting abundantly. We were *one* river, flowing together, yet having started as brooks and streams unnamed. In the midst of incomprehensible trauma, our specific identities had merged into a larger collective Self, and thus we survived what should've been our demise.

Hours later, they loosed our chains and took us above deck once again. Pale people stood along the coast, waving at crewmen they apparently knew. In this landscape, there were no big floral blossoms or rolling hills in the distance. Just land covered in forest. We sighed and looked around, despondent. We were tired of crying. All our tears were spent. There was no use jumping in the water. Where would we go? We thought of uprising, but there weren't enough of us left to fight. So we hung our heads and waited.

As the ship neared the coast, more people gathered. Mostly men, it seemed, but a few women lingered among them. Suddenly the ship stopped. Crewmen assembled around us with guns and bayonets. They spoke quickly words we did not understand. Then, in groups of six and eight, we were forced into canoes that took us ashore. There we stood until all of us had been transported. Pale buyers circled, examining us like cattle for sale. A few considered running. We saw flight in their eyes. But there was no point. We were too tired. Standing was difficult enough. We had been on that ship for months. We'd counted days, but they were not exact, as sometimes evenings and mornings blurred. Still we knew many, many weeks had passed. Without sufficient food, we were again becoming shrunken and frail. Some were obviously ill. Some carried in their eyes the look of exhaustion. A few leaned on others to keep from falling. But the Wolof man stood firm and solid, like a soldier prepared for battle. His stance would be costly, we believed, since pale people whispered more about him than any of us. He didn't care. He would not be bound again.

Even the earth had changed. Our soil was grainy and light brown. The soil here was clumpy and dark. The Wolof man scooped a handful and rubbed it slowly, letting it crumble between his fingers. He shook his head. This was not our home.

We were herded into a nearby structure. It smelled of cow manure and rotten flesh. Men were placed in one holding pen, women in another. It was made of wooden planks held together with steel pins. The floor was covered with prickly hay. All eyes avoided all others. Nothing was familiar. Even our shame was different. On the boat, we had dwelled in relative seclusion, so our humiliation was ours alone. Now, on land, pale observers frowned and scowled as if we were the carriers of something evil. They seemed different from the ship's crewmen. They dressed more neatly and carried an air of sophistication that increased our embarrassment. Were these their *babas* and *umis*? We tried to cover our privates, but being pushed and shoved made that impossible. Some pale people turned away when they beheld our nakedness. Then we turned away from each other.

This was the Coming.

. . .

Throughout the night, we squirmed and grumbled. The Wolof man sat in a corner and stared at us. His eyes said so many things. He would not serve these people for the rest of his life. Or even for a day. Whether in his own land or thousands of miles away, he was still a warrior, and he wanted the world to know it. The rest of us were far less resolute. A few still dreamed of home, surely, but by now their hope had dissolved. Most of us simply wanted to know what was planned for our lives. We still wondered if we'd be eaten. Treated like animals and penned in their stalls, we considered the possibility quite seriously.

When the sun rose, captors entered and shuffled us out. We marched past small wooden buildings where people obviously lived. We marched past edifices we could not identify. We marched until we reached what appeared to be the center of the village. People were all around, viewing and studying us. Even the Wolof man couldn't hide his alarm. He bit his bottom lip to keep from trembling. They had given us strips of thin cloth with which to cover ourselves, and now we stood, bunched together, in the center of a foreign land.

What came next can hardly be described. They grabbed the Wolof man and stood him upon a raised structure. He looked at us, then at them, and back at us again. Pale people spoke all around him. Then, one by one, they explored his flesh. They pried open his mouth with bare hands, searching inside as if he were hiding something. They rubbed his chest and arms, nodding with approval. Then they stripped away his loincloth and gawked—both in awe and embarrassment. The Wolof man frowned and covered himself with his hands. Buyers forced his hands away so that the people might examine him unrestrained. One touched and shifted his privates with a stick, grimacing as if his penis were a nasty, vile, filthy thing. The Wolof man huffed and growled. On they went, lower, exploring his thighs, calves, and feet until they stepped back with obvious admiration.

The Wolof man wept with rage as pale people negotiated the price of his flesh. They waved money and shouted with glee. The Wolof man shuffled in his chains. A pale man stepped forward and grabbed his arm. The Wolof man chopped his throat with the edge of his hand, and the man crashed to the ground, gasping for air. Within seconds, the Wolof man's body was riddled with bullets, but he did not fall. In homage to him, we dropped to our knees. Someone beckoned the gods to come and carry him away. Only then did he tumble, covered in blood, facedown on the earth. We cried freely. His fingers were balled into permanent fists. We believe they buried him that way.

Then they stood Abuto upon the block. He never lifted his head. Someone paid minimally for him and took him away. It was a waste of money. He wouldn't last a year.

Each of us had our turn upon the raised platform. We, too, were poked and prodded until disgraced in full view. Unlike the Wolof man, we did not fight. We had seen what they do to those who fight, so we surrendered and lived.

Our love for each other sustained us. We felt it, in-

visible yet tangible, wounded but living, hurt but not de-
spairing. We stared it into each other's eyes as a tribute
to the battered yet steadfast survivors who would one
day heal the nations. That was our new mission. That
was why we'd been scattered to every corner of the earth.
And, of course, the healer must be wounded to know
the depth of pain. For out of pain comes restoration. We
didn't know that then. Most don't know it now. But the
trees will say it. The wind will send reminders. The rocks
will proclaim it. Clouds will shift in the heavens and announce it. Waves will dash against shores of this new land
and declare it: "These are they! These are they!" until the
dark, beautiful souls of Africa rise and say, "Yes! We are
they! We are here!"

Like broken branches of a tree, we parted ways. If the
aim had been to destroy us, they had failed. If the aim
had been to bruise our pride, they were victorious. Still,
we knew who we were. The secret of our drums continued to reverberate in our souls. The magic of our weaving was still in our hands. The knowledge of God and the
heavens was still in our spirits. We would dance our own
dances again. We would sing songs of our ancestors until
our children knew from whom they had come. We would
call God by a different name, but OUR God would come
in due time. We had endured. We were a changed people,
but we were roots of the same tree.

Even in torture, our souls had not withered. They were buried somewhere deep within, in a place where no person could go. They were as timeless as the sun. Elders had taught us that a person's spirit permeates their flesh, interpreting the invisible and feeling the intangible. Yet the soul never moves. It rests at the center of the Self, as the piece of God that dwells in every living thing. Throughout the journey, our souls fed hope to our consciousness when all hope was gone. It whispered into our weary ears, "There shall come a day when the last shall be first." We believed. We believed because we needed to believe. We cursed our Gods only because we believed in them. Even when they didn't come, we still believed. We welcomed Death because we believed in another life. We ate mush and endured the stench of human waste because we believed we could survive. And we did survive. And in surviving we began to dream. We dreamed so many dreams, we dreamed so many years. We dreamed of our people coming together and building families filled with joy and overrunning with children. We dreamed of someone studying those ships and learning enough to take us home. We dreamed of continuing our initiations in this new land until we were sure we were men. We dreamed of healing rituals that would calm turbulent minds. We dreamed of the pale boy who had loved us from his heart, and we hoped for him a lifetime of blessings. And we dreamed that, one day, our children would know the cost of our coming. That would be enough. That would heal our souls. We had learned our lesson.

This was The Coming.

PART III

We would never see home again. We knew that now. The truth bore down on us like a heavy, massive weight. We didn't know where we were, we didn't know what to do, we didn't know what might become of us. We were strangers in a new land, and we were here to stay.

Soon, we learned the name of the place: Charleston. It felt funny on our tongues, but we repeated it, over and over, that we might never forget. It had been the place of our arrival. Each night in the holding stall, we lay upon prickly hay, wondering who would buy us tomorrow, which of us would be taken away. Some days, after the parade of humiliation, pale men rejected us all, and we were returned to the stall. We then sat huddled together, like a mass of mourning, totally vulnerable to whatever they desired.

Food was little better than it had been on the ship. It was still mush, with a bit more substance and taste. We never knew exactly what it was. We ate it all the same. A few gave it back, moments after swallowing, but they weren't beaten this time. They simply starved. And when, days later, they died, we knew that Death had accompanied us to the stall. He was not as aggressive as he had been at sea, but he would have his due on land nonetheless. Some tried to dismiss him, to send him back to his underground dwelling, but others held him close, refusing to let him go. No one wanted him, but many beckoned him. So Death lingered among us, materializing whenever summoned.

Day after day, we sat in the stall, whispering our fears, then marching to the block to expose ourselves to gray, green, and blue eyes. That was the totality of our lives, the extent of our world. They poured water into a wooden trough at the edge of the stall, and left us to drink like mindless cattle. Most waited till dark that our shame might not be exposed. We wouldn't have drunk at all except we'd chosen to live—and since water is the sustenance of life, we bowed and sipped until our thirst faded. After drinking, we wiped our mouths, sat in a circle, and spoke in hushed registers of our tongues:

"What will they do with us?"
"Can we get home from here?"
"How do they know what we're worth?"
"We have to fight! We can never give in!"
"Maybe some of us will be bought together."
"We're not animals! They can't treat us this way!"

And on, until most had spoken something. A few said nothing. One young man had not opened his mouth since leaving home. We did not know the sound of his voice. Tears poured with the rising and setting of the sun. He stared into the sky each day as if seeing what he'd left behind. Sometimes he'd smile and nod, and sometimes he'd gather into a fetal ball and rock as he trembled. We watched, hoping he'd stay among us, praying he wouldn't summon Death and go with him. He was a slight young man, hardly the weight of a water gourd, with a complexion so dark he melded with the night. Many spoke of his remarkable beauty, his unblemished appearance, and pleaded with him not to surrender. He looked into their eyes, but made no promise. An Asanti man called the boy Nyaméama, which means "What God has given, no man can take away."

Pale people passed our stall each day, peering and pointing at our cursed lot. They saw us. They saw our eyes. They knew our longing. They knew we wanted freedom. But none would help. No one was kind enough even to offer bread or a sympathetic hand. No one gave a nod or a look of respect. They just stood there, staring at us, imagining, surely, how we'd increase the quality of their lives. Our yearnings meant nothing to them. Our pleas of distress went unheard. Even if they had understood our tongues, we believed, they wouldn't have helped us.

We stopped counting days. There was no need. We were too far from home to return. Some said seasons had passed. It was cooler than it had been at the beginning of our journey. The air, especially at night, was frigid and sharp, puncturing our skin like a thousand needles. Warmth came only from the huddle, so without fail, we bound together as the evening sun disappeared. We twisted and wiggled until our meshed bodies blurred together and ignited enough warmth to keep us throughout the night. Someone's head lay buried beneath another's armpit, someone's feet vanished between another's legs. We were a matrix of human parts strewn together in survival. Someone, someday, would tell our story. Of that we were sure.

We wondered about Abuto and Chisanganda. Would they find love again? They would certainly not find each other. She was in another land, far across the sea. He was somewhere here, somewhere near, but we didn't know where. And wherever he was, he was certainly no one's servant. His only hope had been Chisanganda's heart, and without that, he would give God's breath back. We sighed. If he wasn't dead already, he soon would be.

A pale buyer bought Nyaméama the next day. He stood upon the block like a statue of grief. He was groped without shame. He was lean but muscular, and pale hands seemed unable to resist him. He looked at us, one last time, and this time, his eyes said he would live. They said thank you for the comfort, for the whisperings in the midnight hour, for the reminder of his majesty and power. He'd almost forgotten who he was. Almost let the devastation of the journey erase his past. But now he remembered. And he would never forget.

They draped him in chains. He could hardly walk. His buyer dragged him away as the shackles sang a sad, dark song. We hear that song now, in the depths of our souls, and we think of that young man who looked like our nighttime sky, and we pray he never stopped looking up.

This was not the end. There would be another day.

• • •

As for the rest of us, we waited our turn. We were about fifty in number. It was only a matter of time. Some bright morning, a pale man would come and buy us and lead us away. We tried to imagine where they took us but, like our bodies, our imaginations were bound. We saw others of our people, accompanying pale ones to and fro—women with baskets upon their heads but no joy in their eyes, men tending horses and laying stones as if the men were mindless objects—and we knew, whatever this life, it would not be *our* lives. It would be our strength in service of *their* lives. Still, we chose to live, for in living, there was hope.

Rainy days were miserable. In our huddle, we shivered and tried to avoid cold streams falling from the shabby rooftop, but everywhere we moved, raindrops followed. We settled for a far, dark corner where only light mist and weaker streams drizzled upon us. Men spread themselves around women, shielding their bodies and their virtue. It was a small comfort, but a comfort nonetheless. We'd been unable to do this on the boat. Now, on land, we tried desperately to become what we once were—men of valor and stature. Women did their part, too. Whenever sickness crept in among us, they spoke it away, using their hands and voices as instruments of healing. It was the only reason we survived.

Day by day, others were sold off. Our hearts hurt so badly we rubbed our chests to keep from collapsing. At home, we'd never known loss like this. Certainly people died, but mostly elders. We were prepared for their transition. We'd been taught that it was the natural order of things. We even longed for details of the invisible realm. Elders warned us not to be anxious for such knowledge. We would know soon enough. When, rarely, a young person died, we understood that their work on earth was complete. It was a sad occasion, surely, especially when he or she was beloved, but still there was purpose in the movement so we understood. In that holding stall, we did not understand. People died each day and were dragged away like insignificant stones. It was not divinely right. It was not ordered by the heavens. It was not sanctioned by the ancestors. It couldn't have been. There was no joy in the passing, no celebration of life, no clarity of who these souls were and why they'd been sent. Or why they'd survived at all. There was nothing but confusion. And our hearts, lying heavily in our chests, bore it all.

We learned quickly the few names we didn't know. The men were Babatunde, which means "The spirit of father has returned" and Temitope, which means "Give thanks." There was Diji, which means "He tills the land" and Nkiraka, which means "The best is still to come." There was Koofrey, meaning "Don't forget me" and Hassan, meaning "Handsome and born first of twins." His identical brother, Ata, had been tossed into the sea. Of the women, there was Monifa, which means "I am lucky" and Kaya, which means "Never go back." There were two tall, thin women with bulbous eyes named Jaha, meaning "Dignity" and Ayodele, meaning "Joy has returned." There was Afia, which means "Born on Friday" and Nkechi, which means "Of the spirit of God." We did not inquire of their tribes. We cared less about that now.

Our preoccupation was with our own failures. We

mumbled regret for having ignored so many proverbs. We shook our heads about lessons we'd deemed useless. We wept for having disregarded, that fateful day, the sense of danger lingering in the air. We pleaded for forgiveness for having assumed ourselves invincible. It was the only reason they overtook us. We were simply off guard. And when a community is off guard, it welcomes disaster. We knew this. We'd had warrior traditions for centuries. We'd also had gatekeepers posted at the edges of our villages, intercepting anything or anyone potentially dangerous. They warned of the pale man's presence, his love for deceit, his willingness to destroy life to get life, but his innocuous introduction betrayed us. We'd been impressed by what he had. Now we wanted none of it.

Our sorrow multiplied. Without movement, hours were long and torturous. Someone mentioned uprising, but it was impossible. There were no weapons, and we had no strength. Also, unlike aboard ship, pale men did not dwell nearby. They came only to take us to the selling block and return us if we remained unsold. We were captive in a stall unfit for the foulest beast. It smelled of manure, feces, urine, and death. We tried hard not to breathe, but of course that was impossible. Occasionally, someone attempted conversation, hoping to keep our spirits revived, but usually their words had no effect. We were not in the mood for talking. Most days, we peered through cracks in the wall at people and things we'd never seen. All we wanted was to go home. We told our gods we understood. We'd learned our lesson. But they didn't agree.

So we sat and endured. Sometimes we touched each other lovingly. Such was never rejected. We rubbed hands, heads, feet, arms, and backs until at least some comfort was achieved. We knew only each other's names, but it didn't matter. We shared fates, so other details seemed unimportant. We didn't care about favorite colors or the number of rings in one's ear. What would've been the use of such knowledge? What we knew was that we were alone. We were all we had. So, through touch, nods, and talking eyes we encouraged each other to hold on until we discovered what this life might bring.

This was not the end. There would be another day.

. . .

Fifty dwindled to forty. Horses and wagons carried them away daily as we wailed. Not until then did we know that some pain dwells in wretched silence. It's called Agony. It finds a resting place in the soul and takes residence as if it belongs there. And it never leaves. It lingers like part of the body itself. It makes room for itself, and settles in like an invisible disease, moving about at will, reminding the host of its deadly presence. If, per chance, one forgets its existence, Memory causes Agony to live again. Its weight is unbearable, although it has no physical substance. It can lie dormant anywhere it chooses then suddenly resurrect, bringing the carrier to his knees. It has no cure. Even time has no effect. Indeed, it grows over time, becoming more excruciating by the day. The only way to survive Agony is to coexist with it. And, so, with each person sold, we crumbled to the earth and wept as Agony eased into our souls. Then we rose and returned to the stall as if we'd simply had a nightmare. We could have seemed divided in our affections, but we were not. Had we given Agony full reign over our spirits we would've died instantly. But we wanted to live, so we gave Agony its due, then let it settle and wait for another day.

Because of Agony, we could not sing. At sea, our home was just behind us, closer even in our minds. We bemoaned our shortcomings and promised, in our hearts, a victorious end to this tragedy. Our melody, then, was our strength, our sustenance, our battle cry. We believed we'd win. We believed we'd see our people again. We believed pale men would feel, ultimately, the wrath of a mighty people. Yet in the stall, those hopes dissolved. Some believed we'd get home, but most didn't. Some still boasted of warriors, but most declared them gone. Some said our gods would come, even if it took a lifetime, yet most said that was too long. So when one or two tried to hum, no one joined in. It was sad that so many had lost faith. Or perhaps we were simply despondent. Either way, we refused to hum. Hope hid in the crevices of our being and would not show itself. So all melody went mute. In the midnight hour, we let insects have the air, and we listened to their discordant cries while our own rumbled in the bowels of our empty bellies.

We didn't sleep much. We never slept all at once. Our fears allowed only intermittent slumber. Plus, bondage taught us never to close both eyes. Someone was awake during every hour of the night. Often, it was so still we heard our hearts beat. And rats rush across our feet. Yet we were too devastated to care. We knew that, at any moment, we could be snatched away so we tried not to be caught off guard—again. We took turns watching over each other. Sometimes, during the night, watchers would whisper in secret:

"Shall we survive this?"
"We will survive. We always have."
"But never anything like this."
"True, but we are more than we know."
"Maybe we aren't."
"We are."

And, just like that, the exchange would end and both faces turn away. When one would give up, the other would provide encouragement enough to dismantle despair. In this way, the nights crept by. We heard voices sometimes, loud, drunken slurring voices, and saw forms stumbling along cobbled paths but, of course, we said nothing. Their merriment, framed by our misery, was always curious, as we wondered how human beings bypassed suffering so easily. Perhaps that had been our error. To ascribe them humanity they'd never proven. The ancestors were right. Our lesson was not over. Yet if they weren't human beings, what were they? They walked and talked and breathed as we did. Of course, they were humans! They were simply blind ones. They could see only their own people as precious, only their own as worthy of liberty. They, too, were in bondage, but of the spirit. And, sadly, they didn't seem to care.

Each morning, sunrise left us disappointed. As children, we'd sat at the edge of the village, with gatekeepers and farmers, anticipating the moment bold light dashed across the sky. It thrilled us to watch night escape at the threat of day. When the sun eased onto its throne, we marveled that this ball of fire could scatter light all over the world without consuming any of us. Most days its rays were so bright we'd have to squint to observe it. We played a game called "chase the light" where we'd hide behind small trees and run as streaks of light moved with the sun's rising. After many years, we could predict moves so meticulously we'd jump to the exact spot where light landed. We knew even that it moved differently depending on the season. Nature was our playground. It teased our senses and taught us the essence of God. We rarely wasted time with objects. Instead, we bounded around trees and across open plains as our minds tried, though ultimately failed, to understand the mind of God.

In the stall, when the sun rose, our spirits diminished. Another day meant another loss. Rays of light broke through cracked walls and warned us to get ready. Someone would be gone by sundown. It seemed that the sun was weaker here—not nearly as bold and brilliant as ours had been—or perhaps it was our joy that had weakened. Either way, the sun's rising brought dread instead of ecstasy, and we longed for the day when, once again, light brought delight instead of dismay.

This was not the end. There would be another day.

. . .

Babatunde died in the stall. Something he ate disagreed with him. For days, he vomited an orange-and-brown liquid substance, and the whites of his eyes turned yellow. Healers, the few young ones among us, did not know this malady and therefore could not cure it. They spoke to it, urging it to loose its destructive hold, since Babatunde had been good to us, but it would not relent. We'd spoken to illnesses back home and they had obeyed, but they knew us. They knew our tongue, our remedies. This disease belonged to another people and obviously obeyed only their tongue. It gripped Babatunde's stomach and would not let go. We saw his spirit ascend in a cloudy ball just above his head and, within seconds, he took his final breath. We lay him aside, with hands folded over his heart, and we kneeled in a circle around him and clapped and prayed until that hazy, gray ball burst and disappeared into the air. When pale men found him, they tied his feet to the rear of a horse and dragged him away. We do not know where they buried him. Or if they buried him at all.

Others died in the stall, too, and we treated them likewise. Back home, earth that held our ancestors was sacred ground. Children did not play there. Farmers did not plant there. Warriors did not train there. It was divine space and we honored it as such. There was no known reprimand for one who would desecrate our sacred ground for, in our lifetime, no one ever did so. Fear of ancestors was very real and no one is his right mind would've welcomed their wrath. And, anyway, we loved our ancestors with a reverence hard to explain. They were our guides, our spiritual coverage, our invisible warriors, fighting for us in realms unseen. We could not live without them. Crops could not prosper without them. Healing could not occur without them. Wars could not be won without them. They were the cornerstones of our community. They sent signs of things and messages through our seers. They sang our praises before God, we believed, and thus garnered good fortune and health for us all. They were with us now. We knew that. They were simply unwilling to release us from a lesson we'd obviously failed at home. Whether we liked it or not, they were committed to our wisdom and spiritual insight—not our comfort.

We sighed heavily. It would take generations for this infraction to heal, for this breach of human trust to be reconciled. Would there come a day when African children, born here, would have no notion of home? No knowledge of the universe? No respect for elders? No desire for initiation? No concern for burial grounds? No commitment to rituals? No gatekeepers? No warrior tradition? No weavers of sacred cloth? No healers of the spirit? No belief in ancestors? Would there come a day? How would they survive? We prayed never to see that day. Yes, we'd been displaced, but we knew who we were. We were cast down, but not destroyed. We were angry and sullen, but we did not question God's existence. The ability to question is proof enough.

For waste, we bore, in a far corner, a shallow hole in the earth with a small twig. When it filled, we simply dug another. Soon, of course, undefiled earth became difficult to find. The scent returned us to the hull of the ship, where we first knew self-loathing. Just as then, we spit and heaved every particle in our mouths and throats until, once again, we hated ourselves for letting ourselves get into this. We turned our backs for privacy and wiped our hands with straw. We were never clean. None of us. A time or two, they threw buckets of dirty water on us, but it did no good. Without soap and fresh water, we were simply filthy and wet. Our noses adjusted slightly to the putrid aroma, but we never settled into the odor. Often, we pressed our noses between cracks in the planks, stealing fresh air wherever we could. On windy days, we relaxed and gave thanks.

For some of us, like Jaha, buyers haggled endlessly. The seller shouted amounts, and pale men bid until their voices went hoarse. Their excitement exploded. They wanted her. They *all* wanted her. They wanted all *of* her. She was medium size, but tall, with elegant eyes and full, rounded breasts. Those eyes, even filled with tears, dazzled like gems in a clear brook. She was simply lovely. They stripped away her cloth in order to examine that loveliness in every orifice: her ears, nose, mouth, anus, vagina. We turned away. She grunted and moaned slightly, but otherwise did not resist. Someone would have his way with her. He would pay dearly for the right, and he would exercise it for the remainder of his days.

She stood boldly, our dignity, as if oblivious to calloused, searching hands. Bids continued to mount. One man dashed his hat onto the earth in anger. Another hoisted a gun as if prepared to kill. A third stood and trumped every bid offered. It seemed not to matter that he would give a fortune for her. Desire beamed in his eyes. His feet shuffled with unfettered excitement. He even chuckled as he watched other men yield. His joy was that of a child. We tried not to imagine what he'd do with our sister, but we knew. She knew. He knew. It would be horrific. It would tear her apart. But he would do it. And she'd spend the rest of her life recovering from it.

They returned the cloth and she covered herself once again. We never learned the final price. They simply pushed her to his side and she followed him away. Jaha, our sister, our living beauty, gone. We would name future daughters after her. We would call her name each night until all of us were gone. We would never forget her. Yet some prayed their daughters looked nothing like her. They hoped, deep in their hearts, that Jaha's beauty never came again. Not if it solicited pale men's filthy lust. Not it if made them give their entire inheritance to own it. Not if it turned daughters into receptacles of pale men's unwanted seeds. Not if it meant girls never owned themselves again. Beauty became a curse we sought to avoid. Back in the stall, Afia took a small twig and began to mar her face. We screamed and cried, "No! Don't!" but she continued. Rivers of blood dripped from her chin onto her breasts. Before she finished, a pool of burgundy rested between her thighs. We shook our heads. We hated it, but we understood. We did not want this for her, but she'd seen what becomes of dark beauty in the land of bondage. We'd seen, too. She'd be blemished for life. But, hopefully, prayerfully, unwanted.

This was not the end. There would be another day.

. . .

There were thirty-five now. The most preferred had been bought. We struggled between being unwanted and not caring that we were unwanted. They didn't even look at us. They simply frowned at our deep blackness and shook their heads and went away. Most often, we were returned to the stall in silence.

Days passed this way. Some days, they didn't come at all. It was as if they had forgotten us. There was no food, no water, no buyers. We shrunk in size and determination. A few encouraged us not to let our spirits fall, but they had already fallen. We had no word for consistent despair. We'd never lived lives of continuous sadness. We'd never known weeks on end with no joy at all. Yet we knew it now. We'd also never known that sadness could be felt in the flesh. That it took form sometimes and ached like an internal bruise. We'd simply never lived with gloom. We knew grief because we knew loss, but grief dwells in the heart. Gloom dwells in the soul. It dampens the fire of life and makes one believe that all happiness has ceased. It casts a shadow over the eyes, causing sunny days to appear cloudy. It suggests that life is not worth living. That death is better than anything life can give. In our minds, we knew better, but in our souls dwelled this deadly thing. We couldn't shake it. We didn't want to sing. We didn't want to eat. We didn't want to dance. We didn't want to talk. We didn't want to fight. We just wanted to surrender and move into the invisible. But our gods wouldn't take us. So we lay upon scratchy hay, waiting for pale men to decide if someone wanted us.

There was one talker in our midst: Temitope. He was short and deep brown, not black like the rest of us. His brows were thick and unruly, and his eyes sat far apart. Beauty was not his blessing, but we loved him no less. And his tongue never tired. When he fell silent, it was only from our urging. His name meant "Give thanks" and he meant to do so, even in the land of captivity. Day and night he whispered of the majesty of God and the truth of our glory. His tongue irritated many, so his voice fell to a murmur but he never quieted. "God is God of the universe," he said. "He is God of this land, too, and He shall redeem what pale men have disturbed." Many didn't want to hear this. Our situation did not confirm his sentiment. Still, he spoke with clarity rare as a white tiger. He was the only reason gloom did not consume us. Even when we chose not to hear him, his voice tumbled through the air, never letting us forget who we were and where we'd come from. Sometimes he even laughed. Not from glee, but because he believed earnestly what he said: "This is not the end of the story. The end shall justify the beginning."

Sometimes he walked away from us and spoke to the air. We were too frustrated to hear, but he was not discouraged. He knew who he was. He knew why he'd been sent. Both to the earth and on this voyage. And, come what may, he didn't intend for pale men to have our souls. So he spoke into the atmosphere, and words became particles that permeated our flesh. We stayed this side of life because, as Temitope babbled, gloom weakened its devastating hold. We didn't know this then. We know it now. We thought that, magically, our spirits rebounded and resumed the desire to live. But in adversity there is never magic. There is only faith. And it was his faith that bolstered our failing spirit. There was no other explanation. We saw the bottom of life in that stall, but we didn't succumb because Temitope believed in us and said so every day and night. Gloom skipped over him although he'd been with us the entire journey. He was an air child, meaning one whose spirit was never heavy. So he called upon the air to carry his message to our souls when our ears could not hear.

And sometimes he spoke to the earth. On hands and knees, he'd press his mouth to the ground and mumble quietly. We didn't know what he said. Most didn't care. They were too consumed with misery. But a few noticed and wondered what exactly he was doing. He'd rise occasionally and clap with excitement as though understanding something we did not, then return to the position of humility. We believe now that he saw our future and understood why things had to be this way. We believe that, in speaking to the earth, he assured our ancestors we would survive. And we would understand. One day. We believe that Temitope saw beyond the moment, and knew that our dispersal around the world would be to the world's benefit. He was centuries ahead in consciousness. Of course he despised what happened to us and how we were treated—he spoke that fury, too—but he seemed less concerned with pale men than with keeping our spirits aligned with our past. The day he took the block and some old pale man bought him for almost nothing, we sighed and shook our heads. He murmured the entire time they twirled and touched him. Then he smiled as they took him away. We did not understand.

Not until we returned to the stall. There, the resulting silence almost killed us. We had not comprehended, much less appreciated, Temitope's effort. It had been his voice that had kept us from total anguish. His words had fought for us. They had shifted the ether. They had re-arranged devastation looming in the air. We had forgot-ten the power of the spoken word. We'd been taught this. Every elder had said it: *Be careful what you say. Words ex-alt or ruin lives.* We assumed that, among a strange peo-ple, words lost their authority since language could not be understood. Our assumption was naïve. Years later, we realized what Temitope knew: The power of speech does not rely upon meaning. Words carry energy all by them-selves. They vibrate through the air, with the intention of the speaker, shaping consciousness and touching hearts whether understood or not. In our case, many shared Temitope's tongue; we simply didn't want to hear him. Positive speech was an irritant in the midst of misery, so we begged his silence that our sorrow might be rever-enced. He turned from us, but never from his mission. Often he paced across spittle, vomit, and mud, dragging chains behind him, declaring, "We shall live! We shall live and not die!" Sometimes he repeated it for hours. The day they sold him away, we heard him finally. His words lingered in the air. They teased our troubled minds. They soothed untouchable places. And in his absence, without conscious consent, we believed him at last.

This was not the end. There would be another day.

• • •

There were thirty-four now. For days, no one came. We were still chained and bound in the stall, but it appeared as if we'd been forgotten. We'd wanted to be forgotten. Perhaps, then, one day, our chains would rot away and we'd simply walk out. Unnoticed, uncared for, unobserved. But that didn't happen. Instead, we sat for numbing hours, avoiding eyes and conversation, listening to the sound of the pale people's world. Horse hooves clanked constantly against the road, and men's voices tumbled through the air. We noticed that, unlike at home, we heard no children. In our villages, on any given day, children's shouts and cries filled the air. There was no end to their merriment. Whether playing games or questioning elders, they stood as the announcement of our abundance. They were never silent. Even at night, they screamed as boys chased girls and girls feigned disinterest. There were far more children than adults in our village. In every village. Each age set consisted of thirty or forty children who belonged to everyone. They roamed the earth as if it were their inheritance. Indeed it was. Elders taught that land, animals, trees, rivers, everything in nature was theirs. Not to own, but to coexist with. In the stall, we heard no children. We knew they existed—we recalled the pale boy on the ship—but we didn't understand their calm. Didn't they play games and dance beneath the sun? Didn't they run about, meandering between trees? Where were they?

And what of their women? Back home, ours could be heard, any time of day, laughing around cooking pots or weaving looms. Their high-pitched cackling reminded men that they were not to be dismissed or ignored. Their voices dominated public gatherings and incited fervor in ritual places. Whenever men attempted to silence them, they were never successful. Most regretted the effort. In collective unity, women's power was impenetrable. Their voices echoed like hunting hyena. When children sought their mothers, they did not go home; instead, they paused and listened for her, among the chorus of women, and, without fail, found her. Certainly some were more vocal than others, but all understood that their strength and influence rested on their tongues. In the stall, we hardly heard their women. Sometimes a small, chirping voice would invade our listening and we'd assume it to belong to a pale woman, but even then we weren't sure. What we knew for sure was that pale men ruled this place. Others fell silent.

It rained again the day they returned. Some of us, dripping wet and shivering, assumed the block as our teeth chattered. We thought such conditions would hurry our sell, but they did not. Shielded beneath contraptions that kept them dry, pale men took their time, once again, examining our flesh. One of us, Ayodele, stood on the raised platform for more than an hour. Her breasts shimmied as she shivered. She tried to cover herself, but they would not allow it. They wanted to see her. They watched her with intrigue. Some even pointed and gawked. Rain hid her tears, but not her sobbing. She hated the way they looked at her without looking at her. She hated the frowns of pale women, as if this were her desire. She hated that obviously they deserved to be dry while she was wet. She hated their lust for black flesh. She hated that her men could not help her. She hated that her women could not hold her. She hated that her name meant "Joy has returned" yet she couldn't find any. And slowly, unintentionally, she began to hate herself for being what pale men desired.

She drew a large price. We knew because the final

bid made others gasp. The buyer was a short, stumpy, pale man with wide, shameless eyes. He would never honor our sister. We knew that. With her beneath him, he would become something disgraceful, something vile, something disgusting. She would be forced, like so many of our women at sea, to bear his weight and perhaps his children. On ship, those who conceived tried to send babies back. They reached into their vaginas with their fingers, hoping to sever the connection between fetus and womb, only to discover that the bond was usually out of reach. Some were visibly pregnant in the stall. Like Monifa. Her protruding belly could not be hidden. Crewmen had used her body as a plaything, and now she carried someone's offspring. She wanted to love the child, at least the part that was hers, but how do you divide a living thing? How do you love one part and seek the destruction of the other? And which part belongs to you? This was a mystery with no answer. Elders once spoke such complicated riddles, training us to think past the confines of simple things, but this enigma rested well beyond anything we had ever conceived. Monifa never spoke with the joy of a mother. She never considered names and meanings. She never wondered which ancestor might return in her child. She simply sat, most days, rubbing her protruding belly, trying to figure out how to erase the pale man's blood in her child's veins. Her distress was in knowing she could not. Boy or girl, her child's complexion would be diluted. Her perfect blackness would not be its inheritance. Every glance at the child would remind her that it had not been conceived in love—the way a child is supposed to be conceived—but in violence and force. Still, it was hers.

Monifa also bore the shame of having no husband. We were not a people to welcome children without communal consent. One did not bear children alone. Such a decision solicited great reprimand and caused immeasurable shame, both for the girl and the boy. But mostly the girl. She bore the child. She literally carried the act within her. It was not balanced, the public disgrace, but it was so. Usually the two were forced to wed. Then, when the child came, we celebrated it as if it had come right on time. In one instance, a young girl became pregnant and refused to marry her suitor. She was shunned and silenced for a lifetime. No other boy ever looked at her. Most other women avoided her. She lived out her days with a beautiful, yet rejected little girl, whom elders called Awiti, which means "The child that has been thrown away." Her mother, however, called her Chiamaka, which means "The spirit always knows." Most of us didn't call her anything.

When the short, fat, pale man led Ayodele away, Monifa declared, "My baby shall bear your name! And you shall live forever!" We wept as the self-declared sisters waved good-bye. In the stall, before her sale, Ayodele had spoken to the child and begged its forgiveness. She lay her lips upon Monifa's belly and asked the baby who she was and why she had chosen to survive. Each day, Ayodele never failed to acknowledge the child with some sort of gesture, whether speaking to it directly or asking ancestors about it. It would be a girl, she'd said. She'd seen her in a dream. She was the color of sand, but bore her mother's features. She would be Mandinka like her people. The day Ayodele was sold away, she kicked and squirmed in the womb. It was not yet the child's time, but Monifa feared she would come. And she did. By nightfall, Monifa lay upon her back, moaning and screaming in labor. When the child came, a girl as Ayodele had predicted, she was white as clouds. Her eyes, however, were deep, dark brown, the color of rich, fertilized soil. She belonged to us. She bore pale people's color, but our features. She bore our spirit, too. She'd come weeks too soon, but she was not weak. She looked around as if recognizing the place. We'd prepared for her to be fragile and frail, but she was neither. She was small though, barely the weight of a coconut. Still, we knew she'd survive. Even amidst deplorable conditions, she'd come to stay. As promised, Monifa named her Ayodele, and each day we watched her grow.

A week later they were sold away. A pale woman stood before Monifa, marveling, it seemed, that mother and child had survived such unspeakable circumstances. She petted the baby's head and scowled as if it were something nasty. Then she studied Monifa's eyes. When Monifa turned away, the woman grabbed her chin and forced their staring. She saw something in Monifa and wanted to own it. She wanted the baby, too. Whatever was in the mother was bound to be in the child, she assumed. So, with her husband's permission, she made the first bid. Others challenged immediately. She topped their offers. They bid again. She offered more. Her husband frowned. The bidding escalated. No one would yield. But the pale woman meant to have Monifa and little Ayo if it cost her everything. Her last offer went uncontested, and she clapped with a toddler's joy. Monifa looked at the rest of us and nodded. We nodded in return. We would never see each other again, but we would remember delivering her daughter, our daughter, on the floor of that stall and watching her fight to live. That fight became our fight. That fight became our courage. That fight became our silent mantra to live and not die.

This was not the end. There would be another day.

• • •

We were thirty now. Nkiraka, a young man who had jour-
neyed with us across the seas, began to speak of what
he'd experienced on the ship. It came suddenly, his voice,
seemingly out of nowhere. He'd been quiet for the most
part, like all of us, but the day Monifa was sold away,
he began to speak. His was a soft, peaceful voice, almost
like a whispering wind. He had large, bulging lips, beauti-
fully curved like mountain ranges, and wide, flat nostrils
that flared with every breath. Back home, he would've
been the envy of every boy in the village. His long lashes
would've made women gawk and whisper with desire,
and he would've been the father of many children. But
not here. Here, in the stall, he had only himself. Or so
he'd once believed. Never could he have imagined what
he'd lived through. Such things had no referent in his
imagination. But he knew them now. And it had taken his
mind all this time to catch up to the tragedy in his heart.
We did not understand everything he said, but we captured most of it: "They tied my hands and feet to separate posts. It felt like they were trying to pull me apart.
One of them stripped away my cloth. The others clapped.
One of them brushed feathers across my buttocks and
blew into my ears. Hard as I struggled, I could not get
free. They were teasing me. They were preparing me for
something too awful to describe. Then, one stood behind
me, saying things I could not understand. I felt his breath

on my neck. I heard him rustle with his pants. Suddenly, he buried his flesh within me. I yelled, but to no avail. It felt like I had been divided in two. My skin crawled. I shuddered with pain. But that only excited him further. My eyes lost focus. I beckoned Death, and he came. I saw him, from the corner of my eye, dancing wildly, waiting for me to decide if I were really going with him. I didn't want to, but I wanted to. The violator moved in and out of me, back and forth, shouting things that made my spirit quiver. It hurt too much to cry. Tears wouldn't have comforted me anyway. My pride dwindled. My flesh ached. I closed my eyes, hoping to disappear, but the crewman's rhythmic abuse could not be ignored. When he finished, my flesh shuddered. I was only half conscious. They untied me and dragged me back to the hull. They slung me onto the plank and chained me once again. I did not fight. I had no strength. I had no pride. I could not find my spirit. It had hidden itself from me. A hole this big"—he cupped both hands together—"lingered inside me. I wanted to vomit, but I had nothing to give. Death lay next to me all night, but he wouldn't take me. I asked why not. He said I didn't want to go. My name wouldn't release me."

We nodded and gave thanks. He shook his head and wept. Nkiraka meant "The best is still to come." Some of us wept, too.

As our numbers declined, we became desperate for each other's presence. A few spoke more often, like Nkiraka, but most simply held hands or rubbed shoulders. We sat close enough to know we were not alone. Bondage was its own cruelty, but not knowing our future was the greatest torment. The same questions billowed in our minds each day: Why do they want us? Why are we here? Why did they do this? Who are these people? How do you sell a person? Under what spiritual authority do they act? What kind of life will we have here? Is this bondage forever? Will any of us see home again? That there were no answers was our daily anguish. All we could do was sit and wait. We'd never been so dispossessed before, so devoid of life's knowing. All we had were ourselves and our names. And each other. And, slowly, as we were taken away, we clung to one another as the last vestige of home.

Nkechi bore a small anklet of cowries and colored beads. After Nkiraka was sold away, we took turns touching that anklet and remembering home, which, now, seemed a cosmos away. Our bead makers were people of extraordinary precision. They carved beads from small stones and other natural objects that would not break easily. They spent weeks rounding and smoothing tiny balls, forcing holes through them that we might string them and hang them from our necks, ears, and noses.

Then they colored them every color imaginable: blue, green, red, black, purple, gold, white, orange. With these, we announced our beauty to the world. We decorated our bodies and pranced before the universe with the pride of human beings. Cowries complemented these beads. They were precious ornaments, used sometimes as currency, but most times as body decoration. Creative arrangement of cowries, whether in a necklace or head-dress, was a skill for which some were highly praised and handsomely compensated. Most people had cowries. Some called them *nzimbu*. Others called them *kurdi*. A few called them *simbi*. But any village of status boasted of them and wore them with pride. Nkechi's anklet bore only ten; still, the very sight of them reminded us who we were. She'd been a dancer, she said, one of her people's best. She was thin, like most young women her age, and walked with the grace of the giraffe. Chains and captivity did not destroy her smooth, easy gait. We commented about her glide every time we shuffled to the auction block. Most of us stumbled along unable to maintain balance, much less rhythm, but Nkechi's steps were leveled and ordered like the stride of the guinea fowl. She was the master of motion, and we marveled whenever she moved. Aboard ship, when forced to dance, her elegance could not be hidden. Even when trying not to dance, her body responded to the makeshift drumbeat

and the movement of the waters, and she gestured un-
knowingly. Her long, elegant limbs, which we admired,
although pale men didn't, hung loose from her torso and
swiveled with supernatural ease. In the stall, she rocked
back and forth throughout the day, dying from immo-
bility. Sometimes she counted rhythms in her head and
beat them out with her fists. But she never danced. She
said the earth wasn't right. It wasn't *our* earth. It didn't
carry ancestral vibration. It didn't give when she stood
upon it. It remained hard and rigid when we walked, as
if it didn't know us. She also said she needed a drum.
A real live *djembe*. She needed the call and invitation of
rhythm to compliment the dance. It was the only way she
knew to do it. To dance without the drum was like walking without feet—painful and impossible. She shook her
head at the thought. And, anyway, how could she dance
while chained? Our movements required absolute liberty of motion. At best, she had a two-foot range. Any
dance she attempted would be a modification of its original, and that she could not bear. So she sat among us,
twisting and shifting like one with a nervous condition.
Dance was in her blood. It was in her belly. It was in her
bones. It was in her being. There was no life without it. If
she didn't move soon, she'd die.

And that's what she did. She died. We woke one
morning and Nkechi's eyes were bulged and rounded like

full moons. Her arms were stretched wide as if pleading with someone to take her. She was perfectly still. All nervous energy was gone. She could dance now, the way she used to dance. She could move now, without limitations of chains and space. She could twirl now and jump as high as the dance required. She was free. She was unbound. She was home.

We circled her body and spoke to her spirit. We asked her to tell the ancestors how we had survived. To tell the Wolof man his lesson had saved us. To assure those thrown overboard that we had not forgotten them. To tell Babatunde that his strength had covered us. And in our mind, we saw Nkechi—tall, dark, lean like blades of grass—dancing sorsonet before the ancestral council while they looked on with amazement. We saw her give homage to the drums, causing them to beat more enthusiastically. Without transition or hesitation, she moved into manjani and elders exploded with praise. She'd gotten her life-force back. She'd been reconnected with her purpose. She could dance now forever. Yet her body lay among us. We touched the anklet one last time, and left it there, atop her feet, ready to testify for us when we were no more.

They found her the following evening. As they had done the others, they tied her feet to the rear of a horse and dragged her away. Even then, her arms flailed as if in dance. Her neck moved, back and forth, with the rhythm of the horse's trot. Her hips swiveled like a fish's fin in smooth, easy waters. Death did not rob her essence. It did not strip away her glory. It could not separate her from life's calling. The best it could do was take her body. But as she was dragged away, she proved to Death that she would have the last word. Or at least the last dance.

This was not the end. There would be another day.

. . .

We were now twenty-six.

In the middle of the night, more conversations arose. The world was still. Silence reigned. We whispered intensely and promised subconsciously never to reveal to the sun what only the moon knew. Differences in tongues forced the use of gestures where words could not be understood.

"What do you think they will do with us?" Diji asked.

"I do not know," Kaya answered.

"We should have been more obedient."

"We should have been so many things."

They nodded together.

Diji continued: "What will become of the children left behind?"

"I do not know. Without initiation, they will be lost."

They faced each other, but could not see each other's eyes. They waited. Kaya reached for Diji's hand. He took it willingly.

"We will not prosper here," Diji declared. "Our souls do not know this place."

"We will learn it."

She rubbed the back of his hand with her small thumb.

"Where did we go wrong?" Diji wondered aloud.

"I do not know. Perhaps nowhere."

"It must've been somewhere. Else we wouldn't be here."

They paused.

"Our elders said that sometimes, tragedy comes on its own," Kaya explained. "It needs no provocation."

Diji shook his head. "Not tragedy like this. This couldn't have happened less we missed the signs. There must've been signs."

Kaya sighed and nodded. "Yes. Must've been."

More silence.

"Did you see them kill your kinsmen, your parents?"

"I did not. But I heard them. My mother screamed my name. I screamed hers, but she did not answer."

Diji squeezed Kaya's hand slightly.

"I am her only daughter. Her only child. All the others my mother conceived did not stay. I'm the only one who stayed."

Diji nodded. "I am the oldest of seven. My parent's only son."

They sighed.

"We will make a life here. Somehow," Kaya murmured. "Life begets life. Elders said that, too."

Diji did not respond.

"We cannot give them our Will. They'll own us absolutely if we do. We must remind ourselves of our past. That will be our strength. That will be enough."

"What if it isn't?"

"It always is."

So many have died. So very many.

"Yes. And so many have lived. The dead live through the living."

Diji's head bowed. "I watched my father struggle to overcome pale men. From the side of our hut, I saw them slice his throat. Rivers of blood soaked the yielding earth. I was too scared to run. I stood there, gasping for breath, wanting to call his name, but not wanting to be discovered. Thinking raiders were gone, I stumbled forward, reaching for his lifeless body, when pale men grabbed me from behind. I kicked and swung hard as I could. They almost fell. I fought like the mighty rhino. But, in the end, with guns and nets, they overcame me and chained me to the others. As we marched, I turned and saw bodies scattered across the earth like stray stones. Billows of smoke rose into the air. Our village had been set ablaze. I closed my eyes that I might remember my people the way we were."

Kaya sniffled. "Yes, we, too, were mighty people. We lived along moving waters. When it rained, the river rose almost to our huts. The day they came, it rained. It rained so hard most of us sat still, but we were not listening. Healers said it sounded different, the song of the rain, but we did not hear any difference. We simply heard a storm approaching. Now we hear the difference. The rain tried to warn us that something devastating was coming, but we ignored our senses. They captured us within minutes. It happened so fast we didn't have time to fight. Or scream. Pounding rain drowned out all sound. We wept and called each others' names but our voices went unheard. So many died. Whole families were wiped out within seconds. Death blew his breath over our village. Very few were spared."

Kaya's tears poured. She seemed not to notice.

I alone survived from my family. I and my cousin Kwame. But they threw him overboard with the fever. I am completely alone now.

"You are not alone. We are together. Here."

Kaya nodded. "Yes, together. But still alone."

They said nothing more. Darkness recorded their

voices, but never replayed them. During the day, they acted as if their midnight chat had been a leisurely exchange of lonely hearts.

At the next auction, four were sold, including Diji. He could not restrain his tears. He did not wail. He did not sob. He did not buckle. He did not bend. He simply stood on the block as water streamed from his eyes and flooded his cheeks. Droplets leapt from the edge of his face onto his bare chest and continued flowing. It was a sad sight. The depth of his heart had never been expressed, but we saw it now. It lay in the current swirling in his eyes. We wept because he wept. We wept because he loved us. We wept because, tomorrow, he would be gone. There had been nothing outstanding about Diji, nothing seemingly for which he should be remembered—not until he stood before the world and unleashed a torrent of tears. Then he became our purging, and we understood that the grandeur of his heart could not be spoken. He'd not cried during our entire stay in the stall. He'd simply stared at us, one by one, but withheld the contents of his heart. Now, on the block, looking down at us, separated from his last remnant of home, he couldn't contain his love. He couldn't speak it either. So he said it in a waterfall of tears. We'd never seen a man weep like that. His eyes flushed red as water poured. With every bid for his body, he blinked and said good-bye. He studied each of us, without exception, that we might know his hope for us. At this, the final encounter, he exposed a heart so naked, so pure, so loyal we shook our heads. Our capture had not destroyed Diji's clarity of our majesty. His name meant "He tills the land" and now we knew why. He planted, that day, something deep within our spirits. He reminded us that we were beautiful people. Even in bondage, we had not lost our glory. We had lost our land, but not our glory. That's what Diji saw that day, peering into our saddened hearts. He saw our glory. And it was mighty. It was wounded, but not powerless. It was longing, but not faint. His tears testified that pale people had not touched our essence. They had shifted our bodies, but not our spirits. We were still who we were. Some had said it before, but his declaration was memorable because he never stopped crying.

We do not recall his price. No amount was enough. No offer honorable. They shoved him off the block and he collapsed, but he continued to stare. Tears never stopped flowing. He turned and walked backward, behind his buyer, weeping and shaking his head as they shuffled away. His eyes were embers of passion. Streams of living water paid homage to our survival. And from that day till this one, we have never been the same.

Our hardest night was the day Diji left. We couldn't stop crying. His tears had unleashed wailing in our souls.

We couldn't restrain ourselves. In the dark, we sniffled and whimpered against our will. Diji had freed us to feel. To know. To love without shame. To embrace the fragile, unspeakable, invisible part of ourselves. The part no man could change. No tongue describe. No writing instrument explain. No melody soothe. Our hearts were naked and vulnerable. Diji had broken fallow ground around our grief, and all we could do was weep. We lodged this feeling deep in our consciousness that we might never forget it. It was love unadorned. Unconditional. Unqualified. Unreserved. And captivity had exposed it.

We were drained for the next three days. We slept more than we had slept during our entire stay in the stall. It was as if the world stood still. Some kept their eyes closed even when awake. Some kept their eyes open, even when asleep. Some gathered their knees to their chests and rocked all day. Some stared into the sky through spaces between planks. Some drew images on the ground with their forefingers. Everyone did something. Diji had returned us to our humanness, our godness. He had taken us deep within, to a place that demanded truth. We could not resist. We were feeling people. We'd once been unafraid of our hearts. Now, we'd tried to avoid them, fearful that they would devastate us but, after three days of purging, we knew why dry earth beckons rain. And, in our hearts, we gave thanks for Diji's calling.

After those days, nature sent restoration. We woke to a pair of yellow, black, and white butterflies fluttering easily. They rested on a splintered plank jutting from the wall. We watched them, all of us, as a sign descended from the gods. They did not fear us. Their wings swayed gently, back and forth, like creatures on display. We admired their beauty, their quiet majesty, their stalwart dignity. They reminded us that pale men did not own everything. Not *every single thing*. Not the birds nor the grass nor the moon or the stars. Not the seasons nor the rain nor the thunder nor the field's grain. They wielded power over our lives, but they could not own us. They could not purchase our breath. Our love. Our beauty. God gives those freely. To every living thing. Had we captured the butterflies and held them in our hands, they would be no less wondrous. Their color would still astonish. Their easy way would still confound the wise. Their wings would still carry power to lift them. We saw that. But if bound, would they know it? Would their faith in their beauty remain if others did not see it? Would they surrender the will to fly if their space was limited? We wondered.

Soon, they began to perform a halfhearted dance. One pounced upon the other, the other moved away. One was clearly the aggressor although the other seemed not to mind. They could've been siblings, we thought. Or lovers. Either way, they were together, a pair, living in harmony. They were a moment of magnificence in the midst of immeasurable misery. They were a glimmer of hope in a bastion of suffering. They were a band of believers in the company of skeptics. For a while, a brief, solitary while, we lost ourselves in their splendor. Their grandeur absorbed our consciousness. They played without concern for the surrounding devastation. We loved them. We loved their freedom. We loved their assumed beauty. We loved their indisputable loveliness. Each flutter celebrated clarity of purpose and pride in themselves. Against a dismal backdrop of dull gray, black, and brown, their yellow and white dazzled. Subconsciously, we huddled beneath them, staring at what we used to be. They must've felt our admiration. They hopped about in a small circle, but did not fly away. Up closer, we studied the specificities of their makeup. White spots decorated the edges of their wings. Streaks of black lay between large slabs of bright, shining yellow. Even their tiny bodies were black with white spots. Hairlike antennae extended from their heads, moving about whenever they moved. We wondered how a worm had evolved into this. What happened in that cocoon to produce something so breathtaking? Of course, no one knew. But maybe, one day, someone would ask the same of us. Perhaps future generations, the beautiful ones unborn, would wonder how we survived it all. What would we say? Or, more probably, what would history say for us? It would not speak truth. Not *whole* truth. It *could* not. What we endured would never be believed. The average head refuses to comprehend traumatizing testimony of the heart. So, as the butterflies took flight and floated away, we sighed, lamenting, once again, our bygone days of glory.

This was not the end. There would be another day.

. . .

We were now twenty.

Those of us who were left had been rejected at least once. For the first time in our lives, we questioned our worth. We'd never questioned this back home. Our value had been well established. Nothing about us was anything but sacred. Now, we wondered what made us objectionable. We looked at each other and tried to understand what they didn't like about us, what the others had that we did not. Yet, we could not discern. So, we sighed and waited.

Just before dark, one cool, still evening, a group of pale men burst into the stall, swinging the door wide. They bore guns and lanterns as if searching for a thief. We gasped and backed away in horror. They shouted words we didn't know, carried by tones we knew well. They wanted one of us. Or perhaps several. The one with the lantern walked forward boldly, grazing eyes across our faces, while those with guns stood behind him, prepared to shoot if we objected. Suddenly he stopped and pointed. Some of us closed our eyes, others covered their mouths and squealed. Two pale men with free hands grabbed our sister, Ifeoma, each by an arm, and yanked her upward. The flesh around her right eye was marked black from a strike she had received days before when the Wolof man fell. In that moment, she bowed like the rest of us, in humbled respect but, unlike the rest of us, she spoke in her tongue, weeping the while, declaring him the most glorious of warriors. Pale men tried to quiet her, to hush her unleashed speech, but she would not be silenced. Not until one of them slammed the butt of his gun against her eye. Then she calmed. Her mouth continued to move, but no sound emitted. We were glad she wasn't dead.

Now, someone had come for her. She had said very little since the day the Wolof man fell. We didn't want her to go. She didn't want to go. But they had the upper hand, so they dragged her to her feet and bound her with ropes. Some of us leapt, hoping to protect her somehow, but the rifles halted our intention. She was portly and well-made, with thick legs and arms the size of any man's. Still, she

could not fight off pale ones. Her only defense was to surrender, so she feigned exasperation, forcing them to drag
her away instead of helping them by walking. Her name
meant "Her character exceeds her beauty." We found it
days later, her name, etched into the side of the drinking
trough. We reached out and touched it and cried.

The next day, five more were purchased. It was quick
and uneventful. They simply stood upon the block while
pale people made their bids. We stared at them, as had
become our custom, then watched wagons carry them
away. We reached for them, a few of us, yet with hearts
overwhelmed and bodies bound, we couldn't connect.
Left unsold, we were returned to the stall. The weight
upon our chests increased. It strained our breathing. It
hindered our tears. But we didn't want to cry. We wanted
to go home. We wanted to apologize to elders. We
wanted God to trust us again. We wanted to tell our story
and end this horrible lesson.

This was not the end. There would be another day.

. . .

We were now fourteen. We feared who would be last.
Who would sleep in the stall alone, with no soul to comfort? Who would stare into the dark and have the last
memory of this filthy, stinking place? There was no way

to know. We didn't wish it upon anyone, but we all hoped to avoid it.

As day surrendered to dusk, sounds of celebration filled the air. Pale people's voices stirred loudly and strange music blared in the background. We pressed our eyes against cracks in the wall and watched the commotion unfold. There were hundreds of them, it seemed, stomping and stumbling on the cobblestoned path. Many of the men were clearly drunk. They leaned upon women and each other to keep from toppling. They all wore the same clothing as the day we met them: women with cloth up to their necks, tightly bound at the waist, billowing outward and downward to the earth. Men with pants that stopped just below the knee and white shirts with extra-thin, flimsy cloth down the chest. They appeared strange, but in our state we held our tongues.

None of the women smiled. It was men who enjoyed the moment, men who reveled in the occasion. Pale women stood with them, but said very little. Most looked rather somber, we noted, offering fake grins and nods as if wanting only to be left alone. Or to go home. Pale men seemed to treat their women as children, we thought. No wonder they looked so sad.

Soon we smelled food cooking over an open fire. We could not identify it, but it was some kind of meat. We licked our lips and savored the aroma. It carried the scent of heavy spices. Our stomachs growled. We yearned to indulge. In our ceremonies we, too, ate in great abundance. Hunters killed enough game for the entire village. Elder women prepared meat until it was tender and tasty. A league of drummers pounded djembes and djun djuns throughout the day and night. Festivities never ended. Men shared palm wine and other drinks while women danced or socialized. All ceremonies—weddings, funerals, initiations, harvests, comissioning of a chief, success at war—required such display. We were people who believed in celebrations. We gave thanks, every chance we got, for good fortune and ancestral blessings. Pale people obviously did the same. We wondered now if, like them, our celebrations came at our enemy's expense.

When the commotion died, we retreated into the circle. It felt hollow and unstable, but it was all we had. Some trembled. Time was running out. We would all be sold soon. It could be a day or three, but it would be soon. We'd watched the others sold away—some for more than others, a few for great riches—and now our turn had arrived. We peered deeply into each other's eyes, trying desperately to record images of faces we'd never see again. We tried not to cry. Tears only blurred our vision. We hugged so tightly bones cracked. Some couldn't breathe. Teeth rattled. Our nerves were on end. We wondered what they wanted with us, and now we were about to find out.

Suddenly, Olufemi, which meant "God loves me," went to the trough and scooped water with both hands. He returned to the circle, as water dribbled slowly to the earth, and called the names of those who'd been sold away. Each person followed suit, moving counterclockwise until everyone spoke someone's name. No names were forgotten. They even called those who'd died on the ship—if they knew their names. One young man was cast into the sea because he refused to dance. He simply would not submit. His name would not allow it. He'd told another, the night before, that his name was Uzochi, which means "God's way is the only way." They remembered him now. There were others, too. So many others. Like the woman who'd died from the fever. Her whole body trembled for three days. Sweat drenched her from head to toe. Death danced around her, joyously, until she surrendered. But before she went, she repeated something in her tongue we did not understand. She seemed adamant, but we could not discern her meaning. She was the only survivor of her people on the boat. We never figured out what she said, but we named her Ngozi, which meant "She is a blessing." And she was. Every name we recalled we spoke. We reached further back and called names of those killed in our villages. Each name took us further into trance until a few collapsed into the center of the circle. The rest of us continued calling names, over and over, like a chant of healing, until ancestors joined in and assured we'd survive. So many were gone! It seemed like hours before we exhausted our memory. As quickly as we'd begun, we completed the ritual and someone offered a final prayer. We then lay upon one another, panting heavily, touching and rubbing flesh, hoping never to forget what we felt like, what we smelled like, what we sounded like when our voices melded together in unity.

Within an hour, Hassan alone was awake. Staring into blackness, he saw his twin brother, Ata, drift into deep, dark water. He couldn't erase the image. He'd tried to remember him, to remember them, as happy playmates, dashing behind trees and huts, chasing each other and being reprimanded for neglecting chores. He'd tried to remember them as excited initiates in manhood training, having secretly decided which girls they would marry if their father approved. He tried to recall tricks they played on elders by pretending to be each other. But nothing replaced the image of Ata being swallowed in the mouth of the Great Waters. Every time Hassan slept he saw it, and he'd wake huffing and shivering. Ata's face was his own, so the image was of himself drifting, drowning, dying in the cold, black, salty water. He imagined Ata fighting toward the surface, arms flailing wildly, feet kicking against the downward pull, but after several seconds, submitting and floating to a watery grave. Hassan would never sleep a full night again. He apologized to Ata for living without him. Yet, in doing so, he hoped to birth Ata again. There was a legend among their people that when an identical twin died, he came back again in the other twin's offspring. That was Hassan's living desire. But he'd need a wife first. And where would he find one here? Who would marry him with no possessions? How could he marry without completion of his rites? Maybe there was a girl, wherever he was going, who had come from his land and would understand. Maybe she would take him simply because he looked like her. Maybe, together, they could build a life of memories and share them with sons and daughters, and maybe then Ata would come again and they could dwell together, even in this strange land. If not, Hassan would be miserable the rest of his days.

Sometimes, in the dark, he sang softly the childhood song they and other children once sang:

Kye Kye Kule
Kye Kye Kule
Kye Kye Kofinsa
Kye Kye Kofinsa
Kye Kye Kofisa Langa
Kofisa Langa
Kye Kye Kaka Shilanga

Kaka Shilanga
Kye Kye Kum Aden Nde
Kum Aden Nde
Kum Aden Nde
Kum Aden Nde, HEY!

It was interactive in that the leader would sing the first line, "Hands on your head" and children would repeat it and do it. The leader would then say, "Hands on your shoulders" and children would repeat it and do that, too, until touching their waists, knees, and ankles. The last move was performed on the ground. The first child to leap to his or her feet afterward became the next leader. It was most often Ata. He was small and quick, like a leopard cub. Few children could beat him. Hassan remembered that they sometimes played for hours. They seemed never to tire. Elders watched, taking note of physical attributes and vocal skills. If only the twins had known they were in paradise then.

When Hassan finished singing, he saw Ata, again, floating in a sea of blue. He bowed his head and cried while his shoulders jerked lightly.

In the morning, we were herded to the block at dawn. Some had hardly awakened when pale men came and dragged us away. We blinked blurry eyes and stumbled with stiff legs. Pale people were there when we arrived.

They stepped aside as we passed, frowning and covering their noses. One pale woman screeched as if in the presence of something dangerous and frightening. We formed a half circle on the earth before the block. We were unchained, one by one, and shown to potential buyers. If no bid was offered, we were snatched off the block, rechained, and reconnected to the others. Sometimes we were beaten for being unwanted. Yet, given only morsels of scraps and hardly any water, what else could we be? We were lean and unkempt, all of us, like fragile young saplings. But we were not weak. A few saw strength in our eyes. Our eyes could not lie. They told of our power, our resolve, our commitment to survive. So, often, with those of us left, they bid on us not by our countenance, but by what our eyes said. We tried to close them, to bow our heads and hide them away, but some pale men jerked our chins upward and forced our gazes. Our eyes said we were resilient. They said we were survivors. They said we had overcome Death. They said there was nothing we could not endure. Pale people heard and were mesmerized. They murmured and pointed at us as if we were creatures from another world. We told our eyes to lie, to say we were nothing, to say we were conquered people, but they would not. They were truth tellers. That's all they would ever be. So each time we blinked, pale people saw strength and vitality where they'd assumed only weakness dwelled.

That's how Hassan was sold that day. His promise to live and bring Ata back flashed when he blinked. It was a covenant he could not conceal. It was the dream of his existence. Come what may, regardless of the hardships he bore, he would have his twin again. That determination shone in his eyes like brilliant stars at night. We saw it. They saw it. Only he did not see it. But he felt it, and he knew his eyes would not lie. The moment he took the block and lifted his head, *oohs* and *aahs* tumbled through the light morning air and we knew it would not be good for him. And it was not. Bids came from every direction. Light murmuring turned into shouting unlike we had heard in many days. Hassan was thin and of average height for our men, with hardly any muscle tone. But his eyes shone that day like pearls of black onyx. We shook our heads. There was no way to hide them. They spoke his soul's intent. And his soul said he could have his brother back—if he would live and multiply. So as life revitalized his limbs, Death lost all hope for him.

Time passed slowly as pale men made final bids. We stared at Hassan, who stared in return and nodded. The pale man who bought him smiled and dashed to the platform and caressed Hassan, from his head to his shoulders, down his back, across his buttocks, down his lean thighs and calves, to his ankles, feet, and toes. He then studied his purchase, clapping with overwhelming excitement. Hassan never flinched. All he saw in his mind was a son—bursting forth from his mother's womb—with the same face he and Ata shared. That would lift the weight from his chest. That would assure him the ancestors had not forgotten. That would give him strength to live when Death came knocking. That would dissolve the image sinking into the blue abyss. That was all he needed. And he would fight a lifetime to have it.

The pale man led him gently off the block. It was as if he wanted nothing to mar his precious purchase, nothing to damage his newest possession. Hassan did not resist. He looked at us, one last time, then turned away forever. He didn't care where he was going. He didn't care what pale men might do to him. He had a plan, a hope, a vision. If it came to pass, he would forgive the gods and leave everything else behind.

This was not the end. There would be another day.

· · ·

Two others were sold after Hassan. One was Afia, the once-pretty young woman who scarred her face that she might go unwanted. Her tactic did not save her. Instead, it made them want her more. They understood the act as a demonstration of unfailing resolve, and they wanted to own the source of her strength. Confusion wrinkled her blemished face. She'd been sure pale eyes would turn from her altogether in abject rejection; yet, somehow, her deed made them desire her anew. They touched her scars gently, curiously, searching for something within that lent strength to withstand. They turned and twisted their heads, marveling at the pain she must've sustained. Instead of destroying her beauty, wounds were taken as something exotic, something primitive, something ancient, and pale people burst with fascination. Bids rang out in chaotic uproar. Afia looked about, bewildered. We studied her and grimaced. This made no sense. We'd believed they preferred the beautiful among us—those with smooth, flawless complexions and tight, muscular forms. This should not be. No one was supposed to want her. She carried no beauty. She should've been left in the stall to die alone, unbought and unneeded. That's what she'd accepted for herself. She'd settled into this plan like one with a terminal disease. There was no need for ancestral intervention. It was simply her way out. Now, however, she stood on the block with voices shouting from every direction. It was not Jaha's beauty for which they'd paid so dearly. She understood that now. It was their own features on Jaha's face for which they'd rewarded her. She bore qualities more like their own—small, narrow eyes, thin lips, rounded nose—and for that they were willing to pay. In celebrating her, they were loving themselves. They could coexist with her because she was kind to their eyes. Afia's features made them scowl. Yet her ability to desecrate herself—and live—made them believe she'd be the perfect workhorse, able to endure life's hardships without complaint. There was no way to win.

Every bid was topped by another. Raised hands seemed never to tire. Pale men inched forward slowly, without restraint, hoping to win the prize. Afia covered her face and screamed. They didn't hear her. Their own voices muted her cry. Her mutilation had been for naught. She would still be someone's property, and they would expect her to suffer in silence. A large, round pale man made the final bid and joined her on the block. He looked her over as she wailed, unconcerned for her heart, but excited about the strength she exposed. Thinking to test her, he slapped her so hard she stumbled. Afia's hands braced her fall. The crowd cheered. She was not broken. She was not fragile like their women. She was something different, something more than mere womanhood. That's why he'd bought her. He'd already imagined the children she'd bear and the cotton she'd pick and the house she'd clean every day of her life. Now he was relieved not to worry about overworking her. Strength was in her blood. It was who she was. It was why she'd been born. And he would never, ever think of selling her again.

Even to herself.

Others patted the pale man's back as he dragged Afia away. She wasn't loaded on a wagon like the others. She was tied to its side and made to walk as the wagon rolled. We dropped our heads and begged our gods to grant her the strength they assumed she had.

Aminata was the other one sold that day. She'd been a quiet, mild spirit during most of the journey, but fire simmered in her soul. Her breathing, even when she slept, sounded like heavy panting. We glanced at her often, unsure why she always appeared breathless. Air rushed through her wide, flat nostrils like bursts of sudden wind. Her lips never closed. The few words she spoke were in praise of the Wolof man. She'd heard stories of his valor. She, too, was Wolof, although not of the same village, so she didn't know his name. All she knew was his reputation. Her words were hard to understand, but with the help of her hands, we discerned the general meaning. He'd killed beasts with his bare hands. He'd fought multiple warriors and won. He'd leveled trees with one blow. He'd sired twenty sons. He'd carried barrels—not buckets—of water from the river to the center of the village. He'd run full speed, chasing antelope across open plains, and they'd barely gotten away. He was more mystery than man. No one ever challenged him. That's why she was so hurt to see him chained and bound on the ship. He was the pride of his people, and now that pride had been stolen away. But it was not wasted. Aminata sang his praises the day he died. She sang them in the stall. She sang them again when she took the block. Her tongue moved like a flame of fire, and every word she spoke sent an arrow to pierce pale men's hearts. They didn't know her tongue, but they knew her sentiment. One man rushed to the block and clasped his hand over her mouth. Seconds later, he screamed when she bit him. Blood spewed down his arm. Pale faces frowned and turned away. Aminata's rage would not be contained. We'd sensed it, in the depth of her breath, but now we heard it, we saw it, and we knew it would cost her everything. With his unbitten hand, the man punched Aminata's right cheek. She grunted, but did not falter. She paused a brief moment, then resumed her praise song. Dribbles of blood crept from the corners of her mouth, but she would not be silenced. The Wolof man was her only countryman in this strange land, and she meant for someone to know his courage, her courage, their courage before her dying hour. The wounded pale man opened a pouch and lay paper tender on the floor of the auction block. No one bid against him. He balled his fist and rammed it, once again, into Aminata's mouth. She fell to the ground. Blood poured through her teeth and onto the wooden platform. But she was not destroyed. She rose again and continued speaking. We begged her to stop. We knew what would happen if she didn't. She knew as well. But her mind was fixed. There was no life for her here. Her only mission, her last vow, was to make sure someone knew the power of her people. She'd be remembered for what she'd said, she believed, even if she were not understood. They saw her stance. They felt her venom. They saw the shared warrior marks. If nothing else, they would know that no Wolof would serve them. Ever. Not a single day. This included Aminata.

Before the end, she raised chained fists and spewed blood as she said, in her native Wolof, "We are warriors! We cannot be defeated!" The buyer stood before her and lifted his hand once more to strike, but she threw herself at him, and they collapsed together onto the platform. The crowd gasped with disbelief. Aminata kicked and flailed with all her might. She pounded the buyer with chained hands and spread blood across his shoulders. He groaned loudly. Other pale men wrestled him free and kicked Aminata with fury. In unmeasured rage and humiliation, the buyer pulled a gun and pointed it between Aminata's brows. In her last breath, she mumbled, "We are warriors!" Then the blast separated her eyes. We shrieked and trembled. Pale women yelped and hid their faces. The buyer shot her again and again, as if killing any future life she might have. Then, quickly, they tied her chained feet to a horse and dragged her away. A stream of blood followed. We were rushed back to the stall. No one spoke a word. We saw Aminata, standing proudly in our dreams, and we remembered the meaning of her name: "Trustworthy." We never forgot the bravery of the Wolof.

This was not the end. There would be another day.

. . .

We were nine now.

We spent the remainder of the day in trance. No one talked, no one moved, no one wept. We were frozen with trauma. If they could do our sister that way, what wouldn't they do to us? The sun eased through clouds as we sat and shivered. At times we closed our eyes, but we did not sleep. Our spirits could find no relief. We watched strips of light creep across the floor of the stall as images of Aminata flashed in our heads. Some of us were angry with ourselves for not fighting. If Aminata was strength and courage, we were definitely cowards. But if we all died, wouldn't they be undisputed victors? How would we redeem ourselves if everyone went with Death? Our options were few and inglorious. We wrestled, on land and sea, with Life *and* Death, wanting neither completely but needing both inherently. We decided silently, in the stillness of the stall, that both choices carried honor. Both held the integrity of our people. The job of the living was to resurrect the dead; the job of the dead was to invigorate the living. They were complimentary existences. What elders had taught was true—Life and Death are twins of the same mother. Now we understood.

When the sun vanished, we merged into our womb of survival. Still, no one spoke. Some relieved themselves in the faraway corner. Some bowed at the trough for water. Some scavenged the earth for anything edible. But we never said a word. Silence was a memorial to the fallen. It was homage to those who'd decided to pay what we, the living, would pay later. It was defiance, in our minds, of their hope for our submission. It was collective unity among a people displaced and dispossessed. It was healing for our speechless souls. It let us replace something incomprehensible with something palatable, something we could live with. Silence was our only weapon. Without it, we would've been devastated. We would've had no capacity to survive.

In the midnight hour, we could not see our hands before our eyes. There was no moon, no stars, no celestial light at all. Only thick, heavy blackness, like an aura of anguish. We felt it, this mood of desolation, and we tried not to succumb, but it sat upon us until we surrendered. A few drifted off, but most twisted and turned the night long, wanting only the image of Aminata to fade. We did not want to forget *her*; we wanted to forget what they *had done* to her. Yet our memory was too fresh; it would not be relinquished so easily. Or quickly. So we learned to remember only parts of things—the parts that let us believe we would win. We had learned, on the ship, to forget. But this was different. It was a trick of the mind, surely, but had we swallowed even half the truths we knew, we would've choked and died in the stall. Or on the block. Or on the boat. Or in the slave pen. Or during the march. No human mind could've carried the weight of our total experience and lived. So we divided what we knew—and saved some parts for a later recollection.

At the sun's rising, sorrow retreated. We sighed and spoke, finally, in soft, hushed tones. No one mentioned Aminata. We *could* not. There was more devastation to endure, more suffering for which to prepare. A pale man came and tossed scraps onto the ground before us. We wanted to defy him, to leave the crumbs where they lay, but hunger would not be denied. Slowly, we took the morsels and shared them evenly among us. No one refused. In the silence of the night, we'd sent Death back to its underground dwelling. We knew where to find him if we needed him, but, for now, we didn't need him. We would honor Aminata—and the Wolof man and all the others—with our living.

No one else came that day. We sat, hour after agonizing hour, waiting to be marched to the block, but it never happened. The anticipation was worse than the act. The slightest noise made us jump and tremble. We were frazzled and anxious like a grasshopper in a field of birds. After a time, we relaxed slightly, though only for a spell. With every sound, we stared into each other's droopy eyes and breathed deeply. Too exhausted to cry, we simply blinked and nodded. By mid-afternoon, we were holding hands. Distant voices lingered in the air. No one said it, but we all wondered who would be next. It's a bad way to live, awaiting your own or your brother's demise. Yet we had no choice. It had become our fate.

Suddenly thunder rumbled and lightning cracked the sky. We loosed hands and fidgeted nervously. Wind began to blow against the walls of the stall. We thought that perhaps our ancestors had come to set us free and take us home. We were wrong. If they had come at all, it was to tell us we were stronger than our circumstances. We were not convinced. Our hearts were so heavy we could hardly breathe. We did not feel strong. We did not feel mighty. We did not feel protected. We felt weak. Vulnerable. Helpless. Abandoned. Dejected. But we were not willing to give up. Not now. Not after so many had died. We lived to keep their names alive. We lived to remind ourselves of our worth. We lived to see what the end of this lesson would be. We simply had no idea life could be so miserable. We lost someone everyday. We smelled like animals. We lived like animals. We ate like animals. There was no joy in our existence. In our villages, they'd taught that life is only joy—even when it's unpleasant. Yet our lives were far beyond unpleasant. We'd never imagined such grief. Now it was our daily measure. If we intended to live, we'd have to do so with no joy at all.

Wind began to whistle through small holes in the wall. Rain pummeled the thin rooftop like a drum. We drew closer together. The storm raged. We imagined clouds shifting in the sky, although we did not see them. A clap of thunder cracked so loudly we screeched. We saw lightning bolts dash back and forth across the sky. One young man, Oluwagbotemi, offered that a storm was nothing more than gods in conversation. He said his people called the thunder Shango and the wind Oya. They were lesser gods, governed by the supreme God Olorun. Most of us had never heard of this before. He said there were other gods, too, who ruled other aspects of life. We listened as nature made herself known.

A sudden gush of wind ripped a weak plank from the side of the stall and tossed it like a blade of grass. We winced and watched it tumble through the air. "Oya is angry," Oluwagbotemi explained. "She ushers souls from life to death. But when they go too soon, she is offended.

Pale men have offended her time and again. They will feel her wrath one day. And they will be sorry." We nodded along. Unlike us, he had no fear of the storm. Instead, his eyes narrowed as he sought to interpret its meaning. He noticed, on the same jutting plank where the butterflies once danced, a small bird standing completely still. He pointed to it. It glared at us. It, too, seemed unaffected by the storm. He said it had come bearing a message. We waited to hear it, but he fell quiet. More lightning flashed, more thunder roared. Strong wind became stronger. We huddled closer together, prepared for the stall to give way. It never did. It swayed and trembled, but it did not fall. In the midst of it all, we wondered what the bird had to say. Oluwagbotemi closed his eyes and rocked, but nothing came. He had not reached that level of initiation, he said. There were those among his people, the Yoruba, who could talk to birds, but they were all seasoned masters. Much as he tried, he couldn't discern the bird's message. He shrugged and huffed. The bird continued to stare.

Soon, winds subsided but rain continued to fall. Thunder grumbled in the distance. It must be their rainy season, we decided. Ours often started this way. Each day for months, rain would fall, either in the morning or afternoon. Crops grew in great abundance. Children sprang forth months later. Our harvests were usually plentiful. There were years when this wasn't so. Sometimes rains failed to come or came only sparingly. When this happened, we performed rituals of atonement to the earth and sky, and set things aright. Then rains came freely, as they poured now. But there would be no harvest this year. Or the next. What would our people do? Our children had been exiled in our own villages. They, and the very old, were left to forge a life alone. Elders would certainly teach them our way, but they couldn't *show* them, so many truths would be heard but never understood. Most levels of initiation would have to be skipped. Our people would survive, surely, but much of what we had achieved would drift into a glorious past, which they would not experience. We realized this as rain soaked the earth.

And we still wondered what the bird had to say. It looked at us, each of us, with a quick jerk of its head as if dumbfounded that we missed the point. Hard as he tried, Oluwagbotemi could not discern the bird's message. He stared at the winged creature, hoping something magically, something meaningful, might seep into his consciousness, but it never did. He simply didn't know enough. He was only eighteen rains. No one his age back home possessed such power. It would've come much later, if he'd sought it at all. Knowing himself, he probably wouldn't have. Such knowledge hadn't captured his imagination back then. He'd wanted to marry and have lots of children. Nothing else mattered. Perhaps if he'd valued what animal speakers knew, they would've taught him things in his youth. Those things might've been enough now to help him interpret the bird's presence. But he'd ignored such mysticism. Now, try as he might, his spirit could elicit no clarity.

We relaxed our expectation of him. We understood. There was no failing. He couldn't have known as a child that, one day, he'd be bound on the other side of the world and his life might depend upon his ability to speak to a bird. He couldn't have known that a whole host of captives would, one day, solicit his spiritual insight in hopes of being free. He simply couldn't have known. We couldn't have either. But there we were. And nothing we could've done in the moment would've granted us the insight we didn't have. So, eventually, the bird flew away. We missed whatever the message was. Oluwagbotemi apologized for being unable to do what his people did regularly. We forgave him. All of us suffered the same loss. Looking at us, no one would've guessed we came from people who traveled planets and cured diseases with plants and herbs. Instead, they would've guessed we were poor, unintelligent, spiritually defunct people who lacked civilization. This was simply untrue. Yet nothing about us said otherwise. From the looks of things, pale people were the keepers of the universe, the ones who enjoyed God's favor. They ruled land and sea, it seemed, and we had nothing. Not even ourselves. They had bought our very flesh! When we'd had slaves, we'd purchased people's labor—not their bodies! We never thought we owned someone's arms, legs, feet, heart. How was that possible? How much does an arm cost? A leg? Feet? Hands? How did they know the amount of paper money equal to our entire existence? And when did they start this absurdity, this purchasing of human beings? Were we the first? And, anyway, why not simply bind their own rejected citizens ? They had to have them. We'd had them. Every society has them. That way, they wouldn't have to go halfway around the world for what they needed. This was, of course, useless meditation. They had us, and that's what they wanted. Someone unlike themselves. Someone upon whom they could place the burden of their luxurious living. Someone at whom they could laugh without feeling guilty. We were different enough that whatever they did to us they could do without shame. They could justify our abuse simply because we were something they were not. At least in appearance. And such difference, particularly in color, undoubtedly equaled a fundamental inequity in their minds. None of this made sense to us, but we considered it for them since, in any rational way, we couldn't understand their stealing us from our homeland and refusing to let us return. They had to believe something about us that we didn't believe, something that invited them to treat us as men and women without souls. But until we learned more of their tongue, to read and hear what, apparently, they would not say, we resolved to dodge their wrath whenever and however we could. We didn't know what the end of this journey would be, but we intended to see it. Then we would know.

This was not the end. There would be another day.

. . .

The next morning, we were dragged through mud to the auction block. We knew the routine—where to stand, not to speak, not to look pale people in the eye—but, frankly, they were not our concern. Our concern was who'd be next and who'd be last. The crowd was large, despite small pools of muddy water and a cool, crisp breeze blowing regret into our faces. We were huddled near the front, just below the raised platform, and made to wait until all anticipated buyers arrived. Then, one of us, Mawuli, was disconnected from the rest of us, and herded onto the block for all eyes to see. His people were the Ewe, he'd said, a creative people who valued nothing over their ability to speak. But not just speak; rather, to conjure through speech. He was the son of the village chief, in line to inherit the throne. He spoke often of his village's storytellers, of their mastery of language and wordplay. Some of them knew more than a hundred thousand words, he'd said. This, coupled with a cheerful spirit, allowed them to bring stories to life before their people's eyes. Crowds sometimes sat for four and five hours listening to the same tale spun without their ears ever tiring. Yet storytellers were not the only masters of the tongue. The people in general loved the art, Mawuli said, and used it in everyday greetings. It could take two adults several minutes simply to say good morning. "We honored each other that way," he said. "Such was not to be skipped or simplified."

Now, shivering upon the block, Mawuli's lips shifted slightly as pale men made their bids. No one heard him, but deep within, he heard himself speaking to the God of his people. He'd been taught to acknowledge God's grandeur before making any request, so he prayed as his ancestors had prayed: *Mawu, Maker of the sky and sea, creator of life, great and small, master of ideas and riddles . . . Make me to know the purpose of this thing. . . . Give me insight where only anger dwells. . . . Make this lesson known! But if not known, make it knowable . . . that we might not give up hope.*

"Can I get a hundred for this buck? Can I get a hundred? Can I get a hundred?"

All we have now is ourselves.... Can this be enough? Can we bear this weight a lifetime? It is hard to hear you ... but we do not doubt ... They can capture us but they cannot capture you.... Deliver us if it is your will.... We have suffered and survived what, in the past, would have killed us.... We are far more than we know ... and you are far more than we can conceive.

"One hundred fifty, one hundred fifty, one hundred fifty? Can I get one hundred fifty?"

Mawuli chewed his bottom lip: *There is no power greater than you.... No thing more lovely, no one more precious, no being more righteous ... We know this.... But we do not understand your ways.... We know that they are correct, but we do not comprehend them.... You placed the stars and planets in the sky....*

"Two hundred! Two hundred! Will someone give me two hundred for this black boy?"

And you put fish in the waters and birds in the trees ... You are the only thing everlasting ... and we need you now. One lone tear streaked his right cheek. *Cover us until this lesson is complete.*

"Sold! To the man in the back for two hundred dollars."

Mawuli never looked at him. The man came forward, slowly, confidently, and took Mawuli's arm. He did not grab it or shove him the way others had done. He took it strongly but sensibly, like one leading the blind, and walked him to his wagon. There, he nodded for Mawuli to stand and wait. He obeyed, but he did not stop praying. His name meant "Never forget that God exists."

The man returned to the auction and bought two more of us, Damani and Njeri. He led them to where Mawuli stood. Then he unchained them and motioned for them to climb onto the back of the wagon. They obeyed, looking at us from the corners of their eyes. They were sad to leave our womb, but glad to be together. We were happy, too. It was strange, really, our gratitude for being sold together. We'd started out furious at being sold at all; now, simply not being sold alone was a relief. So much of our way of life had changed. We cared less for grooming; we simply wanted to be clean. We didn't think of favorite foods; we just wanted to eat. We didn't care for a soft place to sleep; we longed merely to sleep uninterrupted. Without the torment of nightmares and hungry rats. We saw, in our minds, excess and abundance in our villages, and we wondered if it had angered God enough to spawn this lesson. If it had, we had gotten the point. There was no luxury here, no abundance of anything, nothing lavish at all. The only thing we treasured was each other. But couldn't we have learned this lesson at home?

They sold one more that day: Amma. When they grabbed her, she kicked and swung her arms, but at our protests she calmed. She had been sick with the flux when we arrived, so they had yet to present her at sale. Filling her anus with wax hadn't helped, and every day she'd smelled like feces and vomit. Today, though, she seemed better. Our healers had done their work. So, for the first time, she took the block and stared at hungry, pale faces. Within seconds, she fainted. We screeched and moved toward her, but pale attendants blocked our way. One of the men who'd dragged us that morning approached Amma and kicked her slightly. We winced. He didn't care. He wanted her to rise and be sold. At least for something. Someone passed him a dipper of water, and he dashed it onto her face. She stirred a bit, collecting her consciousness, then struggled upward. Pale women shook their heads with pity. Pale men gazed to see if her struggle was sincere. The auctioneer started the bidding again, but this time much lower. Amma wobbled unsteadily, threatening to collapse again. We spoke strength to her spirit and made her look at us instead of at them. She was Akan, she'd said, and her name meant "Born on Saturday." It also meant, according to her grandmother, "The happy one." While in the stall, too sick to move, she'd spent most of her days etching symbols into the base of the walls. Her people believed in symbols and the power they carried, so they created them for practically every communal idea. One symbol, *adinkrahene*, was a small circle surrounded by a larger circle, which was surrounded by yet a larger one. Amma said the image stood for greatness or royalty. She said it could be found anywhere in her village: on thatched doors, clothing, or upon the ground. She scratched it into the bottom of several planks. It was small, so most would never notice. Another symbol she called *duafe*. It looked like a wooden comb. She said it meant "love everlasting" and "a woman's virtue." Girls often placed it upon their headdresses and sometimes drew it upon their flesh. Still another symbol was called *gye nyame*. It represented the omnipotence and immortality of God. It looked like a human spine with moons connected on both sides. We'd never seen anything like it, but we liked it. Amma said people bowed before this symbol in public. So we bowed. The strangest symbol she carved into the wooden wall was called *sankofa*. It resembled a bird whose head was bent backward toward its tail feathers. We frowned, but Amma said her people took its meaning quite seriously. It was about the power of the past. It stood to remind the Akan that they could always correct their mistakes. It was about the beauty and power of wisdom. How the past functions to help create a glorious, more excellent future. How experiences build insight and help construct sharp perception. In essence, Amma said it meant "go back and get it." It reminded her people that, often, we miss things in life that we later need. Humility insists that we simply return and fetch it. We wondered what we might've missed that had landed us where we were. Amma shook her head. All she knew, she said, was that one day we'd have the chance to correct our faults and we'd see our failings. We nodded. The image of that strange bird looking backward never left our consciousness. Neither did Amma.

They sold her within minutes. They assumed her fainting had been a ploy, a stunt, to distract buyers away from wanting her. So pale men bid even higher, intrigued by one with such talent and strength, especially after having been in the stall so long. Yet Amma had no tricks. She was barely standing. Shy and withdrawn, she'd always avoided crowds, especially the center of them, even among her people. Now, with harsh, unloving eyes gawking at her, her legs promised to give way if she did not retreat. Of course, she *could not*. Instead, she closed her eyes and shuddered. The world around her swirled. She felt as if she were on the seas again. The very ground upon which she stood seemed to spin, and all Amma could do was fight to steady herself. We saw her limp form, swaying like a sapling in the wind, and we prayed she wouldn't fall again.

And she didn't. Pale people laughed as if at a performance. Some pointed each time her body leaned one way or the other. We whispered in our minds across their mockery: *You are the mighty river, daughter Amma. Let your spirit flow! Do not surrender your power unto the undeserving! Stand, daughter of the Akan! Stand!* Amma's spirit apparently heard us for, somehow, she managed to remain upright.

One very bold pale man approached the platform, frowning at Amma as if she were from another galaxy. He proceeded up the short steps and stood before her wobbly form. Without shame or hesitation, he cupped her breasts, each with one hand. We turned away. Unbeknown to us, his eyes rolled to the top of his head as he imagined the ecstasy Amma might provide. Too tremulous to resist, she simply swayed as his hands massaged her breasts gently, then more intensely, before he bought her altogether. She collapsed into his arms. He seemed not to mind. His imagining of her use did not require her consciousness. She could provide precisely what he wanted without ever again being cognizant of her own existence. He carried her to his wagon, in the bend of his arms, as if bearing dead weight. We never got to wave good-bye. We shook our heads as the tattered wagon switched down the winding, dirt road.

Those symbols outlasted us in the stall. Surely pale

men never noticed them, etched into their walls at the level of their feet. But they were there, in undetected glory, prepared to tell our story—if, someday, someone cared to know it.

This was not the end. There would be another day.

. . .

We were now five. Our last day approached. We could feel it. We hoped that all of us would be sold together, or at least on the same day, and no one would be left alone. But there was no promise. We agreed to be strong, come what may. We vowed to search for each other if somehow that became possible. Of course, we wouldn't know where to look. We didn't know where we were. We swore all the same. We spoke proverbs to ease our discontented hearts: "A determined soul shall be made fat!" "Hope retained is hope rewarded!" "God never forgets!" "The wealthy do not always prosper!" "Poor today, ruler tomorrow!" "Sticks in a bundle are unbreakable!" "When bound together, friends become family!" "Do not take what you did not plant!" "Greed loses what it has gained!" "Beauty is never perfect!" "Love never gets lost!" "However long the night, the dawn will break!" And on until we heard our people's voices in our heads. Then we sighed and sat in a small circle, wondering what else to say. Nothing came. Hours passed, slow and brutal. Atiba drew circles upon the earth, Akinyemi stared into the air, Binta played with her hands, Zinzele tried to see home in her imagination, and Olufemi watched the sun's light move around us. There was nothing else we could do. Occasionally we drank water or relieved ourselves in the corner, but always we returned to the circle. It was our last hope. It was the only symbol we shared. It was the only reason we didn't die. We'd all been taught that, in a circle, there is no beginning, no end. Energy flows without ceasing. One can enter and exit without ever disrupting it. Something magical happens when people gather in a circle. Individual identities swirl into a collective self, which wields far more spiritual force than any one person alone. We knew that. And though small, our circle of five did precisely what elders had said it would do.

As evening came, we merged together for the last time. Somehow we knew this was the end. We lay upon each other's bosom and wept for what was to come. If only there was something to say. We wanted to take refuge in speech, but it would not come. So touch was our final requiem. Every hand felt another's flesh. Soon a collaboration of souls ensued and we enjoyed the tranquility of our final night together. We abandoned anxieties of tomorrow long enough to create a memory that got us through the night. We would never forget it. It would be our hope in years to come. Without announce-ment, we simply moved our hands across each other's limbs and faces. Our hands spoke so many things. They said Thank you for enduring. They said, I love you for living. They said Bless you for being. They said We shall see each other again. They said Pale men could separate our bodies but not our spirits. They said Do not become the evil that brought us here. They said Ashe for sur-viving. They said Forgive me for war. They said *Yeabo* for prayers unspoken. They said Our gods have not for-gotten. From dusk to dark, we massaged black bodies until practically every part of everyone's flesh had been anointed. Some moaned aloud as our souls longing was satisfied. We didn't know what tomorrow would bring, but we didn't intend to face it fearfully. We were warriors and healers, storytellers and dancers. We were not people who surrendered—even in bondage.

The hour or two we slept, we dreamed. We dreamed a collective dream. Each of us was there, along with so many others, standing in the center of a land, surrounded by hundreds, no, thousands who appeared to resemble us completely. There were the young, the old, and the in-be-tween. Food sat piled high on tables stretched in every direction. Children laughed and played in the distance. Adults screeched about bygone days. Elders wondered what our future held. Ancestors hovered, just above us, smiling with glee. We couldn't see faces clearly, but we saw every shade of brown and black conceivable. And every size: tall, short, round, thin, husky, hefty, muscular, slender, fat, stocky. These were our people. And they were beautiful. The land looked like our land, but different. It felt like our land, but changed. There were a few pale people in revelry with our people, and we didn't understand, but ancestors nodded approval so we held our peace. Every face lost along the journey was found on a young person's face. It soothed our hearts. It excited our souls. God had kept God's promise.

Then we woke. Everyone saw the vision. Some remembered one part, some another, but it was the same dream. Had it come to tease our wounded consciousness? Or had it come to affirm our decision to live? Either way, it left us confident that this was not the end. There would be a day after today, and in it, we would be multiplied. Yet for now, we had to survive.

When pale men came for us, they were alarmed. We were already standing, lined in a row. Usually they jerked and grabbed us until we were upright and ordered for movement, but not today. When they unlocked and opened the door, we stared straight forward and walked with confidence. Pale men scowled. They did not understand. At the block, we did not shiver. We did not search faces to see if they wanted us. We did not gather into a tremulous, human cluster as we had done days before. We stood, shoulder to shoulder, wrist to chained wrist, and waited. Voices grumbled about the strange, peculiar nature of our posture, but we didn't care. We didn't even look at them. A few approached and studied our eyes, but they did not gain our attention. They were startled and disturbed. Yet that was irrelevant. We'd simply decided to reserve something for ourselves. They could buy our bodies, but not our resolve.

Akinyemi went first. His name meant "He shall be our warrior." He was short, with round features. Pale people seemed not to admire him, but they made their bids and he was off. A pale man chained him to a wagon, and Akinyemi strained to see if someone else might come along. It did not happen. Among his people, he'd been a singer of songs. At every gathering, he said, he and others sang their people's history. His voice was high and chirpy, like that of a warbler bird. Sometimes we'd hear him singing, with his eyes closed, heralding the triumphs of kings, hunters, and warriors. When he realized he was singing, he'd stop abruptly as if having subconsciously violated a sacred oath. We asked him to continue, since his voice soothed and massaged our memory of home, but he would not. His songs were not for entertainment, he said. They were cornerstones of ritual and ceremony for a people who loved themselves and their God. He would not sing them out of context. Not intentionally. We respected his position, but urged him nonetheless, hoping that the intensity of our need might override his conviction. It did not. Occasionally, however, laying upon his back, he'd drift into trance as mellifluous melodies emitted from his throat. We'd freeze, trying desperately to capture every precious note. Sometimes, we'd lean our ears toward his mouth, summoning sounds directly into our memories. His voice recreated our past so completely that often we wept. It sounded like wind blowing through trees. It sounded like the soft strain of the brook. It sounded like easy-flowing rain on a rooftop. It sounded like a chorus of birds welcoming the morning sun. Often, minutes passed before Akinyemi realized he had serenaded the world. We were grateful every time. When he stopped, we sighed collectively as if we'd been holding our breaths. His voice was a sweet melody, a healing song, while we remained in the stall. As they led him away, we heard a bird in a nearby tree sing his praises.

Binta was next. She was thin and shapely, though sickly in the eyes. Too tired to conceal her exhaustion, she assumed the block and dropped her head. Akinyemi prayed his buyer would buy her, too, but another pale man won the bidding. She wept as if tomorrow wouldn't come. She'd tried not to cry, but her heart couldn't be restrained. She was the mourner among us. Not the weeper—there had been several of those—but the carrier of grief. She could sit next to a person and feel their sorrow. It was a vibration, she explained, that moved from hand to hand, hip to hip, like a contagious virus. All of sudden she would burst into tears, leaving everyone astonished and overwhelmed. Then, moments later, when her wailing waned, others would feel cleansed and light, as if some invisible power had washed their souls anew. She'd wept practically the entire journey. Some, she said, could not cry for themselves so they borrowed her heart. It was a difficult life, but it was hers, so she gave her best. Standing on the block that day, we stared our heaviness into her spirit and she took it—without hesitation—and purged what we could not say. There was something absorbing about Binta, something we could not explain. All of us hoped to go with her if with no one else. She knew us without having to know us. One of her eyes was noticeably larger than the other. Pale men undoubtedly assumed the irregularity to be a birth defect or a childhood accident. Each day they rejected her. But there was no defect, no youthful mishap. She'd been sent this way. Without her, many of us would've died of misery. When she looked at us for the last time, we saw in her eyes the eyes of God—perfect in their imperfection—and we smiled. She smiled. Her name meant "She is always with God." She would go with Him alone.

Someone bought Zinzele and Olufemi together. They were blessed. In years to come, they would be forced to mate and bear children who, like them, would be worked into an early grave. Yet for now, they were glad. They were young, too—hardly eighteen or nineteen rains—and far more able to bear disappointment than the rest of us. They believed that in going together, they were recipients of God's grace. And they were. In their future hours of gloom, they sought each other and avoided the bottom of sorrow. Yet they would know hurt in the loss of all their children—the premature, the beaten, the sold away—and, in the end, they would have only what they had in the beginning—each other. Zinzele found herself pregnant every year for the next twenty-five years, and Olufemi believed he'd fathered only six of them. Their love dwindled into functionalism, and when Death came, it came for one in the spring and the other in the summer. But they didn't know this then. All they knew was that wherever they were going, they were going to-gether. That was comfort enough.

This was not the end. There would be another day.

. . .

And, finally, there was Atiba. He didn't care who bought him. He just didn't want to remain in the stall alone.

Not by himself. Not with Death. A night in that place
would kill him for sure. He'd lived among his people, the
Fon, back in his village. He'd dwelled and suffered on
the ship with kinsmen he'd learned to love. He'd sat with
survivors in the wooden stable and decided to live. And
now he couldn't imagine life on his own. Without someone to touch. Someone's breathing to listen to. Someone's words to settle his rage. Anyone. Just not Death.
Death was a poor companion. He didn't talk much. He
loved to taunt and mock the weak of heart. He had a way
of shifting and moving that left others unsettled. Sometimes, without permission, he'd evoke laughter at the absurdity of life and, suddenly, take one's breath away. Just
like that. No, he couldn't dwell with Death. And who
else was there? In the darkness of the night, he could feel
ancestors and speak to them, but they wouldn't come.
Death came easily. He came whenever summoned. He
even came unsummoned. And he hated leaving alone. So
Atiba begged God to send him somewhere. Anywhere.
Just not back to the stall.

When the bidding began, he looked among the
crowd. They were hungry for obedient black flesh. So he
gave it to them. They had scowled at him before, but not
this time. He knew what to do. He'd learned what they rejected, what they hated most. So, unlike before, he wore
the look of sympathy. That was the submission they had

wanted, the surrender they'd been after. An expression of joy would've been disingenuous. Happiness would've looked unbelievable. Bliss, inconceivable. Love, unthinkable. Contentment, unsustainable. These realities didn't move them. All they sought was his compliance, his acquiescence. So Atiba yielded. In exchange for the loneliness of the stall and the provoking of Death in the midnight hour. He conceded, in exchange for death without libation or life without elation. He assumed the mask of passivity and pale people pitied him. That was the only expression of love they knew.

Among his people, he'd been the trickster. The time bender, the reality shifter, the mind regulator. At every ritual he'd been called upon to illustrate the depths and dimensions of the Fon. He'd acted out people and situations, causing even chiefs and governors to laugh at themselves. He'd mimicked voices and behaviors so precisely others marveled in awe. He'd worn costumes and recreated war battles that resulted in solutions elders could not find. His talent was becoming everyone else in order that the community might see itself. Now, here, in another place and time, in a much more desperate hour, his skill would save again. But this time it would save himself.

Pale men smiled and nodded. Atiba bowed. A few women applauded, as if an achievement had been realized. Bidding escalated. The crowd inched forward with pleasure. Atiba held his pose. They began to touch him sensually, first his feet and ankles, then, on the platform, his head, chest, and thighs. All the while Atiba sneered. It wasn't a broad, welcoming grin, but a slight, meek, concessionary smirk that made them believe what they had once only assumed: He needed them. He wanted them. He was grateful for them. And for that, the bids went higher. Atiba went further in the performance, studying not only their eyes but himself behind their eyes. He was a thing to them, an object of their ownership, and if only he could accept that, they would love him. But he would never accept that. Yet he knew, now, that if he acted like he did, and his *vodu* favored him, he'd get the same reward.

The winner was a tiny pale man with an even more petite wife. They approached the platform, arm in arm, smiling at each other, sure that their purchase would do them well. They were wrong. Atiba would take their lives in not many days. And he would do so with the blessings and authority of Mawu-Lisa, the Supreme Being. Yet for now, they each took his hand and led him to their cart. He was too kind to chain to the side, the wife protested, so he rode in the back, chained to nothing but himself.

No one knows what happened to the stall. If pale people ever saw the symbols or felt the presence of Death dwelling there. We were simply glad to leave it. Most of us never communed again, but we remembered the womb that birthed us, this part of us, and we told generations stories of our survival. There had been so many of us in the beginning. Then, slowly, our numbers dwindled. Some were tossed into the sea. Some died from fevers. Some took their own lives. Some starved to death. Some went with Death willingly. Some were killed in uprisings. Some were sold at the first port. Some died from the flux. And some perished from a broken heart. Those who made it to the stall were only a fraction of the whole. And, one by one, we were distributed across a strange land to service a strange people. Each day our numbers declined until, one day, Atiba, the last man standing, discovered the secret of prosperity in the land of bondage. He was the last of our womb. He would plant the seeds of our return. In our souls, we remembered him. In our hearts, we praised him. In our spirits, we thanked him.

This was not the end. There would be another day.

This was The Coming.

READ ON FOR A SNEAK PEEK AT DANIEL
BLACK'S BREATHTAKING NEW NOVEL

LISTEN TO THE LAMBS

Listen to the Lambs

Beneath the intersection of I-20 and I-75, where stray trash tumbles about carelessly and dreams lay aborted, where coke cans substitute for ashtrays, and discarded, warped, pissy mattresses serve as sleeping quarters for discarded, warped, pissy people—beneath that invisible expanse of earth and sky, dwells a man named Lazarus. Most never see him, but he's a wonder to behold. Short, coarse, stubby black hair covers the lower half of his face, composing a thick, unkempt beard that grows midway down his neck. Sharp, piercing eyes—oh those eyes!—framed by long, elegant lashes, suggest that, under different circumstances, he might've been handsome. People stare at his eyes in wicked envy, as though they don't belong to him or as if they're offensive against such stark, solid blackness. They're lighter than usual, which, on a black man, means striking. Some say copper bronze or muddy brown. Others, russet or cappuccino. A few, golden honey or creamed latte. All agree they're remarkable. And rare. Enclosed in almond-shaped lids, Lazarus's pretty eyes keep others from dismissing him as the useless nigger they think he is. Thick, bushy brows, from which unruly gray hairs spring in every conceivable direction, shield his eyes and rest like grassy mountain ranges beneath a sloped forehead, causing people to glance twice before turning away altogether. A lion's mane of massive, coiled, angry dreadlocks swings from his head in belligerent disobedience. His oval, chiseled face conjures images of masks worn by African ancestors in battle. Meager flesh cloaks his strong, skeletal structure although Lazarus is not thin. People think of him as lanky though not slender, undoubtedly because his strut isn't stereotypically black. There's no rhythm, no syncopation, no glide. It's staccatoed and hesitant, as if, somewhere along life's journey, he lost faith in his feet. And only by his feet, can one know that he'd been meant to be thick and muscular. They appear clown-like, his wide flat feet, as if, in colossal haste or angelic mockery, God attached the wrong pair. Throughout high school, Lazarus wore a 14, but that was decades ago—when his shoes were new and feet manicured. Now, with bunions, blisters, corns, and talon-like toenails, no telling what size he wears.

His other distinguishing feature, besides those pretty, golden eyes, is his ivory-white teeth. They stand perfectly even and ordered, moving, whenever he chews, like disciplined soldiers in a regiment. Upon smiling, Lazarus upsets viewers' initial perception of him as yet another wretched, homeless soul. Many frown with apparent disbelief that a man of his station, with nothing and nobody, actually cares about dental hygiene. Yet Lazarus has vowed never to walk about with teeth so disagreeable they embarrass him. Black gums and brown, half-rotten molars are inexcusable, he believes, when a toothbrush is practically free. Toothpaste, too! At least baking soda. Shit! Who can't get that? *Being* homeless is one thing, Lazarus always says: *looking* homeless is quite another.

Most days are spent watching cars, pickup trucks, and SUV's go by. He imagines the lives of passengers, sitting at Thanksgiving dinners, gorging themselves and laughing around their abundance. Or perhaps fixing plates and going to separate rooms where they enjoy self-induced solitude. Either way, they drown in excess and that's what almost killed Lazarus—the weight of excess—so he dropped it all and never looked back.

It wasn't an easy decision. He'd never dreamed he'd sleep on the streets like some unknown vagabond. All he'd wanted was to simplify things, to stop wasting life's energy on the accumulation of useless junk, but he'd built the expectation, and his family wouldn't release him from it.

Deborah, his wife, didn't understand why hating a job meant quitting it. "After all," she explained, "Everyone hates their job, or some aspect of it, don't they?" Lazarus didn't respond. "What gives you the right simply to walk away?" That's how the argument began. It ended with Lazarus toting a packed suitcase of clothes and toiletries, which, after kissing his son and daughter lightly on their foreheads, he carried through the front door. Deborah didn't worry. She believed his good senses would return. But they never did. He simply walked into another life as if the previous had been a fleeting, momentary thought.

In his mind, he chose homelessness because he was dying. Years of corporate America, wining and dining, seminars and evaluations, left him believing his life was spiraling downward. The harder he worked, the more he neglected his family, the richer his bosses became un-til, one day, he simply said, "I can't do this anymore!" and walked out. The next morning, he woke in a panic. How would he pay bills? How would the family eat? He could've had his job back—He was sure of it!—but he couldn't swallow his last modicum of pride. *Lazurus oh Lazarus* his mother used to sing whenever she couldn't figure him out. She'd always end the melody with a ques-tion like *What's wrong with you, dear Lazarus?* Now, the refrain echoed, like a scratched record, in his memory and reignited longing for a mother he could never have again.

Deborah could have it all, he'd said, although he'd

meant to say she *was* his all. The look of rage, lingering upon her face, made him know that an attempt at reconciliation was futile. He loved her far more in his head than his heart, and once he began to despise his previous life, he despised her along with it. He'd tried to separate the two, the life from the love, but the day he quit his job and Deborah didn't understand, the two entities blurred into one lump of disgust.

The real reason he quit was because he lost everything. Overnight, just like that, the economy bottomed and when he woke, his life's savings had dwindled to nothing. Every month, hundreds of dollars had been drafted into 401ks and money market accounts, and suddenly his hope of financial security was gone. Dissolved. Vanished. It didn't matter that others lost everything, too. They weren't him. They didn't know what was at stake for a black man who had risked everything, who had trusted America, who had done the *right* things. Now, he didn't know what to do. But he knew for sure he wouldn't do *that* again. Now he understood why granddaddy had hid cash beneath his mattress. No, he didn't earn interest, but he didn't lose anything either.

The meeting with his broker was quick and solemn. The man assured him the economy would probably rebound—"This is America, after all!"—if he'd just let things be. He understood that the hit was hard—more than 70 percent of his savings lost—but, again, America had had recessions before. Lazarus nodded easily, like a man in trance. None of the words had reassured him of anything, except that he would never work and save like that again. His hope had vanished. His faith was gone. The word of his broker's that rang in his consciousness was *probably*. That was enough to seal his resolve to go in another direction, live a different life. And that's what Lazarus did.

He sat in his office in the dark for the next three days. He didn't bathe, he didn't eat, he didn't say a word. He simply pondered why he'd spent his life working like a mule. Was he trying to prove something to himself? To his father? His Grandfather? His mother had warned against it, saying, "One day, son, when you have your family, spend time with them. Don't let them long for you." He hadn't really understood what she'd meant. His father's contradictory words had taken deeper root: "A man who can't provide for his family is worse than an infidel." He didn't know what an infidel was, but it sounded bad enough, so, at 17, he prepared to sacrifice everything in exchange for comfort and security.

And he did. But now he hated himself for it. His father never said it could slip away overnight. He never said a man could wake one morning and all his efforts be gone. That's how Lazarus felt. That everything he'd ever worked for had suddenly disappeared. His pride had no strength; his ego mocked him in flight. If not for his kids, he probably would've walked out the front door and never looked back. But he'd never leave his kids. That was non-negotiable. He adored them like Christ adored the church. But he'd teach them something different now, something contradictory to the way they'd once lived. It would be abrupt, he knew, and certainly they wouldn't prefer it, but it was right. And if it wasn't, it was what Lazarus now believed, so it was what the family would do.

He didn't worry. Lazarus IV, called Quad, and Lizzie worshipped their father. The boy was seven, the girl five. They especially enjoyed when he tickled them until they peed. That was the sign of his absolute adoration—if he could persist until their laughter left them hoarse and yellowy wet. Tired or not, he played the game whenever the children desired, and they felt enormously blessed to have such a remarkably committed daddy. Grown now, and having missed their father for years, they were more pissed than ever.

Yet Lazarus had been looking for something. He couldn't articulate it, but in the bowels of his belly, in every pore of his being, he knew it was out there. The desire had tumbled around in his soul until, at age 50, it simply wouldn't be denied. He discovered that the pain of life hadn't been in pondering things; it had been in not knowing. Thus his dream: to spend his latter years knowing, creating things of substance, constructing a life of meaning. He'd had enough of emptiness and counterfeit joy. He wanted the real thing, and he wanted it now.